Goodnight, Sweetheart
and
Other Stories

Goodnight, Sweetheart
and
Other Stories

by
Richard Teleky

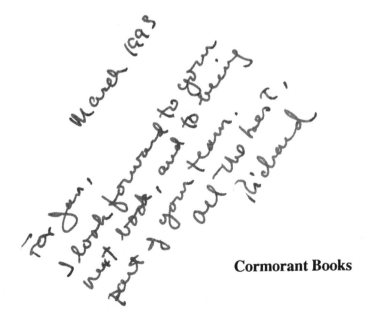

For Jen,
I look forward to your
next book, and to being
part of your team. All the best,
Richard
March 1993

Cormorant Books

Published with the assistance of the Canada Council, the
Ontario Arts Council, and the Government of Ontario
through the Ministry of Culture and Communications.

The writing of this book was assisted by the Canada Council
and the Ontario Arts Council, and the author is grateful for
their support.

These stories first appeared in *New England Review, Antioch
Review, Descant, Ethos, Quarry, Louisville Review, Literary
Half-Yearly, Tamarack Review, Confrontation* and *Crescent
Review.*

Front cover art from an oil on canvas by Gathie Falk,
#8 from a series titled *Development of the Plot,* courtesy of
the artist and Wynick/Tuck Gallery in Toronto.

Cover design by Artcetera Graphics, Dunvegan, Ontario.

Edited by Gena K. Gorrell.

Published by Cormorant Books, RR 1, Dunvegan,
Ontario, Canada K0C 1J0.

Printed and bound in Canada.

Canadian Cataloguing in Publication Data

Teleky, Richard, 1946-
    Goodnight, sweetheart and other stories

ISBN 0-920953-47-6

    I. Title
PS8589.E375G66 1993 C813'.54 C93-090040-5
PR9199.3.T45G66 1993

For my parents

Contents

Goodnight, Sweetheart

I decided to make the film several days before admitting it to myself. "What are you, an all-purpose prophet? Do you really care about that?" friends ask when I get going. Well, I bet there were a lot of things Jeremiah wasn't interested in, but nonetheless.

A dutiful son, I've come home to help. And tonight the house is finally quiet, Grandma's last rampage gone from threats into tears and exhaustion. My father sits, elbows on knees, head hanging. I'm suddenly overcome with love for his years of stupid, passive pain. He's kept silent too long. Simply fell asleep whenever a feeling might have been asked of him. Yet his face is kind and the neighbours' children follow him about when he rakes the front lawn or shovels snow.

I wonder if this is a good time to bring up the film, but decide against it, though earlier today I called my producer at the station, who asked for a "total policy concept." Gary always talks like that. Sometimes he even calls me "old buddy."

"It's a pit," Mother says, heading into the kitchen. "I can't do it."

Mother's idea of a pit is an efficiently run nursing home called the Eldorado, which I visited this afternoon. George Hingley, owner and manager, proudly pointed out a chair with straps that can raise bedridden patients into a bath, the recreation/rehabilitation room, decorated with kindergarten-like drawings, and a cafeteria of plastic tables and chairs that serves as chapel, dance floor on party night, and general assembly place. This is no spot I'd want to spend much time in, but it's far from a pit. Mr. Hingley, who has several decades left before he turns into a resident, assured me his "guests" love him. Just about then I had the sensation of walking into a good property for documentary TV. "We happen to have a vacant bed this week," he added. I told him the decision wasn't mine alone. "Ah, yes," Hingley sighed.

Which leads me to Mother: I close my eyes and know that five years from tonight I'll have perfect recall of Hingley's bushy eyebrows, but my own mother is harder to summon up. Maybe this is true for everyone you love—the face seen in so many angles of laughter, reflection, boredom and irritation that it all blurs into an impression of movement, of life. Like most filmmakers I have a good visual memory, but the best I can do for Mother is an old still shot, at least thirty years old: a young woman's open smile, brown curls tied down with a scarf of daisies; no lipstick, no make-up; yet bright gay eyes and flushed cheeks and the happiness at seeing me climb up our back stairs.

"There's no lemon." Mother appears again, carrying a tray with mugs.

"You aren't seeing, Ma, when you call the Eldorado a pit."

"I can't just abandon her." She's been crying in the kitchen, but has composed her face.

"Dad, try to make . . ." As usual my father shakes his head. "You can visit every day. A ten-minute ride, that's all. Hell, the Eskimos leave their old behind when . . ."

"This isn't the North Pole, Steve. Do you want milk in your tea?"

There's a crash in the back room, followed by pounding noises.

I look at the dining-room clock: a few minutes after midnight. "Why don't you take away her cane?"

"You try," Mother retorts. "If she doesn't hit you with it first."

I tighten the belt of my robe and head into Grandma's room.

"Who is it?" she growls. "Devil!"

"It's me, Grandma. Steven. You must be having a bad dream."

The curses and pounding don't prepare me for the sight of her sitting on the bed, a pink flannel nightgown unbuttoned to the waist and one arm and shoulder pulled out, one naked freckled breast exposed.

"I want to go home."

"Grandma, this is home. You've lived with us since I was a kid. Let's put your arm back in the nightgown."

"Did he send you? The Devil?"

I cross the room toward her but she shakes the cane. "Please, Grandma."

She starts sobbing. "Father," she mumbles. "Come get me."

She hasn't seen her father since leaving Europe at age sixteen, in 1906.

Mother joins me and we watch Grandma. This is what it can be like at ninety. Only five years ago, in my documentary about epidemics, I used footage of an interview in which Grandma describes the great flu scare of 1917. Grandma wasn't cautious, like other ladies in the

11

neighbourhood. She put on a heavy apron, boiled in lye water every night, and went from family to family, wiping heads with rags she later burned, dabbing camphor oil on feverish lips, peeling oranges for those who would take a little food. "Just try," I can hear her say. Then she went home and scrubbed her arms with lye soap. My interview's final frame: Grandma bursting into a self-conscious laugh as she concludes, "Oh but we loved to dance."

Mother gets the nightgown back on Grandma, who now reaches for her cane.

"Don't," Mother whispers. "Please."

Biographical truth can't be had—I think it was Freud who said this. Somebody big, anyhow. But I start imagining all the people who've lived, people who spent their lives suffering—and it's going on this minute—people who'll never hear Grandma's name, while she sobs into her pillow. A film, at least, can show what happens to somebody else.

"I'll quit my job and take care of her," sighs Mother.

"That's stupid." *Fuck the mundane, I want a cross*—this could be our family motto.

Mother flashes a look that calls on love, regret, at least the sympathy a stranger might give, but it has no power tonight, and I feel ashamed.

"I'm a robot. A shell," says Mother.

I see Elaine, my ex-wife of six months; I know that feeling too.

Crossing the room to Grandma's bedside, I try blocking out Elaine's face. "Grandma, don't cry."

After another round of tears and abuse, this time about four a.m., Grandma finally collapses. "She'll be calling for breakfast by six," Mother states, her eyes

12

glazed with despair. "Maybe you're right, but don't start on me now."

I let her remark pass and wash down a Seconal.

It's Saturday, which means Mother won't be at work—she's a secretary in the local hospital. If I move with just enough emotional pressure, we won't lose the Eldorado's empty bed. So I lean casually against the kitchen wall as Mother fries some eggs. Father sits over his coffee, rubbing one spot on his forehead. Remember, I tell myself, he's had two strokes, he's never been assertive, he . . . he . . . he . . . yet I still seem to expect something: a retired man on disability pension jumps up, spins around, and when the dust whirl stops, is seen in a flowing cape, Clark Kent into—oh, give it a rest.

"I decided last night," Mother blurts out, sliding eggs onto a plate. "We'll go to the Eldorado this morning."

"Are you sure that's what you want?"

"What I want?" Mother repeats, setting down the eggs.

"I'm sorry, Ma. I didn't mean it like that." Silence. "I have an idea. At first maybe it'll sound crazy, but there's a lot of people in your position, and their lives must be hell too. What if we tried to reach them?"

A blank stare. Father dunks another doughnut.

"I've got a good producer, and I could direct the camera work myself."

Her eyes cloud with tears. "You're talking about my mother."

"I know, Ma. But this is a chance to say something important."

"Film your divorce," she replies, turning back to the stove.

Better let that pass. "Don't you see, Ma?"

13

"I see, Steve, I see. Is this why you came home?"

Without saying as much, Mother hears my point. I realize she doesn't want to be put in this position, but is superstitious enough to believe that something governs our moves.

An hour later she comes into my room, while I'm rummaging through a box of high-school mementos. She's changed from her housecoat into a navy sweater and skirt, and put on some lipstick. "How would you go about it, Steve?"

"First I'll have to talk with Mr. Hingley. Get him to let us film . . ."

"You want the whole country to see her on TV the way she is? Most of the time not even knowing what year it is?"

"That's part of it, Ma. And I've interviewed her before, when you said it wouldn't work, and she walked off with the show."

"Steve, she was eighty-five then. I wouldn't be putting her in a home if things were the same . . ."

A crashing noise comes from the next bedroom and both of us groan.

"Devil! Devil! Who stole my purse?"

By mid-afternoon Mother has signed up Grandma with Hingley, who suggests we say she's going into the hospital for tests. As we leave his office, Hingley offers to show us the vacant room, a semi-private one on the ground floor. I hope this won't make Mother reconsider.

Women roaming the halls all seem to wear robes in shades of pink, from new baby to dusky rose. Creepy, that colour, on flesh once soft to touch, catching morning light as a man watched his wife slip off her nightgown.

"You can bring a few of her favourite things," Hingley explains. "Some pictures, a small radio. But of

14

course you understand we can't have too much clutter. Does your mother knit? So many of our ladies knit."

"She can't remember how." Mother breathes heavily.

I want to punch Hingley for his sympathetic smile. Why is it that most knowing people have a strong overbite?

We pass a lady who is tied into a wheelchair, her head hanging forward on a broken neck. She wears a violent coral bathrobe, this wounded flamingo, and her few wisps of grey hair are held in place with a piece of pink yarn.

Hingley offers to send an ambulance for Grandma on Monday morning but Mother doubts we'll be able to get her out of the house.

"Don't worry about that, Ma. I'll take care of things. You see, Mr. Hingley, I'm a filmmaker and we're planning . . ." I explain my idea to a fascinated man who doesn't need much winning over. "The Eldorado's a family affair," he adds proudly, a bit nervous, and I find myself almost liking him.

This leaves barely forty-eight hours, so when we get home I phone Gary to explain there's no time for a "total policy concept." I demand cameras, lights, a decent technician by tomorrow night at the latest. Meanwhile, the Devil has taken Grandma's hairbrush and Mother is starting a migraine. I go into my room and begin making some notes, but Elaine nags at my thoughts. What is a woman for, anyway? I don't want to get lost in this: Who behaves worst, who best? Who gets to say, "I was right after all, you didn't really love me, you're already with someone else."

A shouting match starts up in the hallway as Grandma yells "You must have put it there. How else would you know where to look?"

I cross my room and peer out. Grandma clutches her hairbrush, exasperated.

"You put it there yourself," Mother tries to reason.

"And who took my eyeglass case? Somebody!

I close the bedroom door and start on the script. We'll use a few photographs of Grandma to open, run credits over one of those old postcard shots popular before the First World War: a young girl's heart-shaped face, heavy dark eyebrows above yearning eyes, a bowed mouth, thick hair pulled back softly. A familiar picture to me, a childhood icon that meant being grown up in another, more wondrous, time, where ladies wore long white dresses at the seashore and kept on their summer gloves while eating ice cream that tasted of fresh strawberries and real vanilla.

Cut ahead in time twenty years, to several rows of women in printed cotton dresses. Grandma, sixth from the right, stands ahead of her co-workers at Stone Knitting Mill, where she's a dress trimmer and section head. In front of her, a table is covered with large spools of thread, open boxes of buttons, scissors, yardstick, bolt of cloth. All but a few women smile. Grandma's eyes still yearn, yet her face now has the sad nervous look I remember, barely concealing the desire to conciliate something.

Cut again, but now what I can't show is my first memory—sitting crosslegged on Grandma's high bed, between us a drawer full of buttons taken out from her sewing machine. We scatter them over the bedspread, line them in rows, arrange them in circles. Plastic ones, wooden ones, crystal, glass, cloth, in every colour imaginable. Stone Knitting Mill's legacy. I take a green one, my favourite colour, and put it in my pocket as Grandma scoops up buttons by the handful.

Maybe I'd better call Gary again. Maybe we'll improvise all of it.

By suppertime Gary phones. Tomorrow I'll have my cameraman, equipment, lighting technician, in time to film our Sunday meal, a sort of last-supper affair. My presence in the house seems to put Grandma at ease, or on good behaviour, and except for a brief spell of mumbling, she has a peaceful night. Back in my adolescent bed, I feel a rush of confused sexual longing whose raw innocence has nothing to do with any emotions I lived in marriage. Perhaps I'm healing myself. For life after Elaine.

Next morning at ten Gary shows up with Mike Farrell, Sid Greenberg and a van full of equipment. I've worked with all of them before so we settle down amiably. Mother makes plenty of coffee and leaves us to transform her living room into a set: cameras, wires coiling about sofa and table legs, lights carefully placed in proper angles, and strips of tape laid on the rug, marking off areas for different shots. Sid takes out some grass but Gary says "Not now" before I have to.

"I wonder if she's ever tried the stuff?" Sid muses. "I mean, think of it. Ninety years without a toke. Shee-it."

"I bet that's not all she's missed," Mike laughs, adjusting a light.

But we stop laughing as Grandma comes into the room, floats in, almost, with an expression of benign disgust. You're noisy louts, she warns us without a word. "I'm ready," she announces.

"Hey, watch out for that cord," Mike calls.

I haven't mentioned the interview to her, but when Mother joins us, I realize that my work's been done for me. Fate is fate, after all.

Wearing a pale blue sweater over her best house-dress, Grandma sits down like a new driver backing into

17

a tricky parking spot. "It's no good getting old," she sighs. Sid reaches for his camera, and Mike floods the living room with light. Grandma's face seems to collapse as she shuts her eyes fiercely, covering them with one hand. Mother looks away. The light, merciless, pins Grandma to her chair. Mike turns a few knobs and the glare fades, but for one unplanned moment we see flesh defend itself from us, like an amoeba shrinking up before the light of a powerful microscope.

"It's okay, Grandma, you can look now." I cross over the tape line and stand beside her. She opens her eyes, still covered by one hand. "That's Mike over there in the brown sweater. He's got the lights under control now."

I think Mother's going to be sick.

"It's no good getting old," Grandma sighs again, but is cheered by our attention. "Nobody wants you any more. Nobody cares. Sometimes I lie in bed with no food for days." She raises her voice a bit. "If only I went home to Europe, it's not like here. In Europe I knew everyone. My father, mother. We always had a house full of people. Not like this. At home we were all close. Seven of us. And my grandmother. She always chased away the gypsies who came around begging for food. They would eat anything. Once some of them even dug up a dead cow my father just buried . . ."

Sid moves the camera closer, while Grandma keeps talking. "Get her to look at me," calls Mike, tampering with the light. "Over here."

Gary has a nervous smile, as if I'll deliver a film loaded down with immigrant memories, another pursuit after the old country. The audience for that is dying out itself. Instead, I listen to Grandma and think, there isn't much time left for her, and all of it will be spent unhappily.

"Grandma," I interrupt. "What's the use of love?"

She stops, puzzled, though it looks as if an answer's coming. "I'm always alone," she says finally. "When people love you, you don't have to be alone. Wait until you're old. You'll see."

Last night Mother cried, "She'll pull me into the grave with her, so she won't have to be alone."

"Who are these men?" Grandma demands, reaching for her cane beside the chair. "Don't take my picture. First I have to put on powder."

"We're making a film for TV, Grandma. About growing old."

"I know the kind of men they are." She hoists herself up with the cane and I reach out to support her.

"Hey, watch it." Sid pulls back.

"Devil! Devil!" Grandma's cane whacks at the camera.

Mother runs to Grandma, tripping over a cable.

"Bad men." Grandma keeps whacking. I grab a light before it falls.

Grandma lurches forward, passing gas, and a stain on the seat of her dress catches my eye. Mother gasps.

Grandma runs off toward the bathroom, but a piece of turd has already dropped behind her. I look at Sid. "Got it," he smiles.

Mother returns with a roll of paper towel, pushing it at me. "Go on, it's your film. I do this every day." Exit Mother.

I bend to clean the rug. Elaine always changed the diapers in our house.

"I did not," Grandma now sobs down the hallway. I smell something spicy sweet, like incense, and look up to Sid lighting a joint. Bless him.

We start filming again during dinner, a heavy mid-afternoon meal. Now one of the actors, I hope to add a little panache.

"Someone sprinkled poison over my food," Grandma insists.

Sid zooms in for a close-up of Grandma pushing food around. Gravy splashes the tablecloth. Then she smiles at me. "Take some of mine, Stevie. You shouldn't be hungry."

"No, Grandma, you eat it. I'm fine."

Dinner will end up a heavily edited photo montage. From the glum expression on her face, Mother must be contemplating suicide, while Father makes a well of his mashed potatoes and fills it with gravy. Suddenly I realize where I picked up that silly habit, which once drove Elaine from the table in despair. Just when I think of asking the guys to cut and join us for dessert, Grandma looks into the camera. A noise gurgles in her throat and she demands, "I want to be young again."

No one replies, and Grandma slumps in her chair, staring blankly at her uneaten dinner. "No good," she mutters. "No good."

"What is it? What's wrong, Grandma?" Her bewildered voice makes me want to block Sid, who steps forward to pan the mess of food.

Mother returns, setting down a small bowl of vanilla ice cream, which Grandma spoons with no question of poison. I gesture to Sid that he's shot enough film.

"I'm alone all the time," Grandma charges.

"That's not true. I give you breakfast, come home from work to cook . . ."

Grandma cuts off the litany: "Well, you're better than nothing."

"You always say that."

As far back as I can remember, Mother and Grandma have had a mania for correction, which they regularly trigger in each other. "Stop it," Mother suddenly cries. I realize that Sid's still shooting. "Stop!" Grandma joins in. "Oh stop it. Stop it." She pounds a fist on the table. "Do you hear me?" Sid moves away immediately, lifting the camera down from his shoulder.

"You've got to understand," I explain, sure that Mother won't make us leave. Sid's not just any cameraman, he's got a sensitive eye.

Gary takes Sid and Mike aside for a minute, then comes over. "Are you sure you want to go on with this tomorrow?"

"Absolutely."

"Okay, we'll head back to the hotel."

The house, empty except for family, feels curiously the same as it did with my crew around. The camera changes nothing.

After putting Grandma down for a nap, Mother wants to talk. "You must think I'm a nasty complaining bitch," she sighs. "Well, maybe I am. We fight about her slips all the time. Since she won't wear underpants, they get filthy with stains, and when I wash them she insists my detergent's too strong, that's why they're full of holes. Those slips are over twenty years old, Steve, but she won't touch the new ones I buy her."

"Don't, Ma, you just get . . ."

"I feel like I run a private hospital. I work all day and then come home to dole out medicine, cook special meals and hear about new aches and pains. I'm not a doctor. I don't even like bodies."

"After tomorrow things'll be better."

"It's not just Grandma. Most of the time your father's heart's palpitating or his head's full of pressure. I don't know what's next."

Right now I'm not up to reassuring Mother about our plans, but I don't always do things I approve of.

Slumped in his easy chair, Father is snoring, a remote-control channel changer in his lap. Mother looks at him with patience and something harder, drier—contempt? What is marriage anyway, but patience and contempt?

"Before we bought that thing at least he stood up to switch channels. That was the most exercise he got since World War II."

Of course I laugh.

Mother decides on a nap and I grasp at the nearest point, although not necessarily the right one, the one I want: maybe he's filled with endless yearning. Remember him younger, an awkward handsome man with an intense wife he knew he owed loving comfort. Until she admitted her impatience in jokes, perhaps the same jokes Elaine tells my son at this minute.

I turn to my script, and some notes jotted down before coming home. Care of the ageing, prehistoric time, one card reads. Zinjanthropus, Cro-Magnon, the wonderful names almost calm me, we've been around so long. I could use a few of them in the voice-over, but what TV audience really cares about ageing Neanderthals? I put down my pencil.

This afternoon Gary asks "What happened to your grandfather?" and I realized I never think of him. He spent years tormenting Grandma, that's how I saw it as a kid. With effort I remember his smell of booze, sweat and garlic. One image keeps coming back: Grandfather kneels, for some reason angry, while nailing a slat of our wooden fence. After watching him from across the yard, I go over and stand silently, absorbed. He turns. "Who do you think I am, your grandmother? Go on, beat it."

I force my mind back to the notes.

The sky, clear next morning, cheers Grandma, who sings to herself while Mother adds water to a can of frozen orange juice. An ordinary morning, it seems. *Goodnight, sweetheart, till we meet tomorrow.* Grandma taps her cane lightly against the leg of a kitchen chair. *Farewell, sweetheart, sleep with banish sorrow.* I sit across from her. "Come on, Stevie, don't you know the words?" I shake my head. *... sleep wish banish sorrow,* she repeats.

"Grandma, remember the tests we discussed yesterday?"

She stares blankly, called away from the end of a dance sixty years ago. I'm counting on this; we haven't talked, in fact. "At the hospital."

"Oh yes," she sighs, and Mother looks at me, amazed or exasperated.

"And I'm going to take some pictures. Of the hospital, and your room, and the pretty nurses."

... but with the dawn, a new day is born. So I'll say, Goodnight, sweetheart ...

"Grandma?"

"It makes me sad," she murmurs.

"Then why do you sing it?"

Mother sets a piece of toast in front of us.

"I don't need a doctor." Grandma frowns.

"Only some tests," I add.

"Tests! Tests! They just want my money." She grabs onto her cane.

"Your toast is still warm," Mother suggests.

"It's poison. I want ice cream."

"Not for breakfast, Grandma."

"You eat it." She pushes the toast toward me.

"If it's poisoned, I ..."

"Steve!" Mother exclaims. But Grandma considers.

When the doorbell rings Mother shivers, though it's only Mike and Sid, who set up, measuring light, while Grandma wanders off to the bathroom. We hear grumbling as she passes the Devil on her way.

Unaware that these are her last minutes at home, Grandma dresses, helped by Mother, who even brings out pearl earrings. "All my jewels are gone," Grandma resists. Her jewels: some cultured pearls, rosy yellow with age, and a few brooches.

Before we know it, the ambulance arrives. "I used to love driving," Grandma muses as Mother buttons her coat. "I was a good driver, too." She has never sat behind the wheel of a car in her life. In fact, she always got car sick on summer jaunts into the countryside. "Yes," Mother agrees, and her fingers brush Grandma's cheek.

In walks a charm boy who looks as if he's auditioning for the part of medic on an afternoon soap. Whether it's this new face, the camera or buttoning up, something frightens Grandma.

"Come on," I try cheering her. "Take my arm."

She grabs onto the doorknob.

"Here, Grandma. It's okay."

"No!"

"The ambulance is . . ."

"Don't put me away." She backs into a corner of the hall. "Don't put me away."

Mother bursts into tears.

Sid blocks me with his camera as I move toward Grandma. Lights glare.

"You want me to come back later?" calls the ambulance driver.

"Don't touch me!" Her cane's flying.

"I can't do this." Mother jumps as the camera

swings around on her. "Get that thing off of me." She knocks into Mike, trying to get past me and Sid.

I grab the cane and Grandma breaks down, as if it held all her strength. "It's only for a while, Grandma. Everything'll be fine."

Gary, Sid, Mike, the cameras, the ambulance driver and I form a circle around Grandma that shuttles her into the ambulance.

As we pull up at the Eldorado, Sid immediately hoists the camera onto his shoulder and starts filming. Hingley greets us showing all of his dentures. Beside him, a nurse in her early twenties, with a faint resemblance to Hingley—something about the over-bite, perhaps—stands behind a wheelchair. "This is my daughter Gail."

Grandma looks at the wheelchair. "Is that for me?"

Gail nods thoughtfully.

"I'll walk," Grandma says.

Off the lobby, a small crowd gathers to watch the new arrival. Most of them sport fancy robes and slippers, while a few have tied winter scarves around their necks. Mother takes Grandma's arm and walks with Hingley as Gary joins me, and we watch them moving down the stuffy corridor. I notice that Gary's upset but trying to cover it. "What's up?"

"Both of my parents died in a place like this."

Suddenly I remember the nursing-home fire, the inquiries afterward.

When we get to Grandma's room, Hingley explains that she'll have it all to herself for a while, the extra bed presently unoccupied. Sid keeps shooting while Hingley suggests that Mother join Grandma for lunch— "our special guest"—and promises to let me interview him this afternoon.

25

The guys and I walk several blocks to a greasy spoon. One hour at the Eldorado is a pure downer, and we talk about getting old alone. Among the four of us there are six divorces and about eight broken-off affairs, not to mention the women who count as false starts, or the kids on child support. Gary suggests that we all live in the same city after retiring, so we can visit each other in the hospital, while I try to picture nursing homes of the future, with yoga classes and lectures on impotence.

On our way back I step into a nice ladies' shop, pick out a bathrobe for Grandma and have it gift-wrapped.

Near Grandma's room I hear the muffled sound of someone crying. Inside, she sits on a chair by the window, for no reason wearing nightgown and robe in the middle of the afternoon. Sun shines through venetian blinds, crossing her with horizontal bars of light and shadow.

"Where's Mother?"

"I don't know," she chokes, wiping her eyes with the belt of her robe. "Do I have to stay here, Stevie?"

I don't know what to answer. "I brought you a present, Grandma."

"Oh, Stevie, I want to go home." But her eyes spot the package.

"You will. First, let's open this."

I set the box on her lap as Mother comes into the room.

"You shouldn't spend your money on me."

Mother watches, silent. The paper rips easily and we pull out the box, lift off its lid. Grandma looks down at the robe. "It's green."

"Like grass in summer," I suggest.

"Green," she repeats, unconvinced.

Mother crosses toward us. "Why didn't you buy pink?"

26

There is no simple answer for this.

"I just called your father." Mother pauses. "I can't leave . . ."

"Mom, stop it."

"I can't . . ."

"What's wrong?" Grandma asks.

"Everything's okay." I take Mother by the arm, and we go out into the corridor. An old man in a plaid bathrobe nods, then stops to watch us.

"The worst part's over, Ma. At least give it a try."

"Look at her."

There is an old woman holding a box. A mound of torn wrapping paper on the floor by her feet. A freshly made-up hospital bed with lowered railings. Sun shines through venetian blinds, highlighting two violet plants on the windowsill, and the old lady, who sits crying. Stay detached, I warn myself. No other way to help.

"Think of how she acts at home. This is better. Someone will give her a bath every day, she'll have lots of attention. And if she's up all night . . ."

"Mr. Hingley asked if she's combative." Mother looks desolate. "He said it's usually the women who fight."

I can't help but smile.

She looks back at Grandma again, but finally heads home, and I go off to start some interviews. The activity of even my small film crew is enough to send the Eldoradans into a spin. People line up at the doors of their rooms, some waving, some only peering out, and our association with Grandma—word travels fast here—is enough to give her a kind of celebrity status. Through all of it Hingley maintains his gracious-lady smile.

Gail Hingley, plump cheeks glowing, greets us as we end our tour outside the infirmary. Intrigued by our

27

cameras, she's put on more make-up. Obviously we're considered an opportunity. Sid catches my eye and grins as Gail hurries down the hall with a nice rolling gait. She's swinging an enema bag the way most women do their purses. Suddenly I'm following her.

She turns, hearing my gallop, and sometimes, at moments like this, I wish I'd never learned to talk. "Okay if we come along?"

Gail looks beyond me to Mike and Sid and the cameras. "Sure," she grins. I get it now: she's ready to take her place in the line of legendary screen tests. But before you could say "Hollywood," Hingley is beside us, and Gail's smile fades. "Mrs. Fisher's waiting," he cautions. This time she doesn't swing her enema bag.

Hingley offers to help if we need more shots, and Gary thanks him. Then the guys run me home.

"Finished?" Mother asks as I come in. I shrug and head for a scotch. "You drink too much," she continues.

"Probably." I've never been good at a hard-boiled style, but I'd like to be.

Father joins us, staring glumly at my drink.

"Why don't you have one, Dad?"

"How old do I look to you?" he asks, dead serious.

"What kind of question is that?"

"Just tell me."

The glum look returns. Such a question is totally unlike my father, who only asks if I've had the oil in my car changed recently.

"Drink this, it's unblended scotch. You don't ruin it with water." He takes the glass. "You look in your late fifties, I'd guess, because most men your age are either completely bald or grey. But what's this about?"

Father considers, sipping warily.

"Come on, Dad."

"Your father was waiting in the lobby at the Eldorado, after I called him to pick me up, and one of the old women came over and asked when he moved in."

I can almost smell his shame.

"Apparently the woman asked several times, and when your father explained, she grabbed his arm and kissed him."

"You were sexually harassed!" I blurt out.

Father beams, in spite of my absurdity, so this must be the right tack. "In cases of harassment, you know, it's typical for the victim to feel guilty. But she's probably been soliciting newsboys for years. A 'repeat offender,' I think that's the feminists' term."

"Are you planning a film about this?" Mother mocks. "Because you sound like all men now."

"Sorry. I could phone Elaine, as penance."

I leave them, pass the phone and go into my room. I love Elaine, though there's nothing else to do but wallow in her defects.

After dinner I'm glad to visit Grandma. Mother and I pass a number of quiet rooms, where people lie vaguely comatose, until we hit a commotion. Gail Hingley sees us coming and cries "Thank God."

"What is it?" Mother flusters.

Grandma hears Mother's voice and lets out a yelp.

"It's not just her," Gail apologizes quickly. "Tonight everything's going wrong. There must be a full moon."

We look into the room where Grandma shines with upset.

"She was drinking her coffee and suddenly said 'I've had enough,' and poured it on the floor."

"She did that at home, too," Mother explains. "And she doesn't like taking medicine, either."

"I know." Gail taps a pinkish spot on the front of her uniform. "I'm wearing it now."

From outside Grandma's room I listen to Mother's calming. "Why won't he let me alone?" Grandma asks. So the Devil's up to his old tricks again.

"How can you take it?" I ask Gail Hingley.

She looks up at me, as if sorry about something. "I know I'm interrupting your work, but I need to understand. I don't want a film that reeks of sentimentality."

We pause, feeling close, a comfortable bond. "Have you ever wanted to make a movie with stars?"

If only I could resist answering. "Movies today, hell, all the talent's shooting expensive thrillers or whatever else they think'll sell this year."

"I'd like to hear more about it," Gail offers, drawing in her breath.

"And I'd like to tell you more."

"But I've got to dash now."

I head back to Grandma's feeling pretty good about myself, but outside her door my back tenses up. How many years ago was it that I ran into her room and bounced on the bed, tangled in its blankets at the sound of her laughter under the covers? Such Sunday mornings.

Instead of the strong ceiling light, a bedside lamp now shines, dim and consoling. Mother has smoothed sheets, fluffed pillows. Her attention is what Grandma wanted, and she lies calmly tucked under blankets.

"Stevie, you came to see me too," Grandma murmurs. "I don't like this place."

"Did you have ham for supper?"

Grandma looks at me blankly.

"That's what the lady across the hall was eating."

"Maybe it was ham. I don't know. I didn't eat any."

We end up in one of those safe discussions of food, and then Mother reads to us. The Prince of Wales escapes a firebomb, or perhaps it's Lady Di. I'm not really listening: Grandma's the one for royalty. How to film a moment like this and not make it lyrical, or cheap? Every fool with a movie camera thinks he can shoot documentary films. *Cinéma vérité.* Fancy home movies. Not me. Sometimes I don't know how much longer I can turn out films that upset people. Just to get interviewed, given awards? But I meant what I told Gail about Hollywood and megabucks.

By the time I hit my bed, I realize what's wrong: I'm too involved. I keep on thinking of this, and dream about women. There's Crawford, Davis, Stanwyck and Dietrich, and then Elaine, all dressed in sequins and glitter but carrying rubber hoses looped in circles, like police about to interrogate stubborn criminals. "Hurrah!" shouts Crawford, or is it Elaine, who's painted her lips with a fierce magenta bow that warns all men against any soaring, impossible romanticism.

I wake, churlish, gulp some coffee and hurry over to the Eldorado and my crew. Drooler, the bathrobed gent who hangs around Grandma's room, greets me in the lobby. "Where's my girlie?" he asks. A patch of white hair stands on end, as if it's afraid of him.

"There you are!" Gail Hingley calls, rushing down the corridor.

He turns, blissful. "Great party, ladies, great party. Have to dress now, have to get home."

Gail takes Drooler's arm but looks at me. "Are you filming or visiting, or just scouting up some company?"

"Where's my girlie?" Drooler interrupts.

Gail grins as I leave them when we near Grandma's room. This isn't what I expect: Grandma lies on one side, curled into a fetal position, staring at the door. "Grandma?"

At first she doesn't seem to notice me. There's a big coffee stain on the front of her nightgown. "How did you sleep, Grandma?"

I bend over to kiss her forehead and she whispers, "No good. No good."

There's a dark bruise on her right arm, several inches above the wrist. I touch her hand. "How did you get that?"

I look at her other arm, feeling panic. No mark there. "Did you fall?"

"I don't know." She closes her eyes. I've never seen Grandma like this before.

"Maybe you bumped it last night, looking for the bathroom?"

No answer. She draws her arm toward her chest. "Grandma?"

Nothing.

"I'll be back in a few minutes."

I find Hingley in his office, pushing buttons on a pocket calculator.

"Please, sit down," he gestures. "She's a frisky gal, your grandmother."

I remain standing, and for the first time notice a religious calendar on the wall behind Hingley.

"She did a little exploring last night, around three a.m., and it took a while to calm her down."

I can imagine it all, and don't want to.

"This isn't unusual, it often happens with new guests. But your grandmother got up again around 4:30, so it was necessary to pull up the railings and use a restraint on her arm. I'll show you one. It's padded and can't hurt, unless you try to twist it off."

"Which she did."

He nods. "We'll talk to her doctor about a sedative."

Armed with the explanation, I head back to Grandma. I don't want Mother to discover the bruise and smuggle her out before hearing my story.

Sid, Mike and Gary arrive precisely at noon, and Mother follows behind almost immediately. Grandma still lies huddled up, refusing to talk. Though I don't want Sid to start shooting, I ignore my own objections. What Grandma feels now is part of the truth, and has to count for more than scruples. Yet we're mounting an invasion. Mike turns up his lights and Sid shoots a few minutes' footage, while Grandma remains still, unmoving, so that we might as well be filming a woman in her sleep. She must hear our commotion and feel the lights, but has found a small triumph over us, like an angry child who shuts her eyes when someone takes a family picture, thinking this will make her invisible. For a horrible instant I see Grandma's eyes fill with tears, and then realize I've imagined this.

I motion Sid to stop, and Mike lowers the lights. In the hallway they shake hands with Mother, wish her well, all that. This part of the job's finished. "Did you get what you wanted?" Mother asks, a hint of apology, and Gary gestures toward me, saying, "He's the boss."

The boss. What does he know. Though they all call "goodbye" to Grandma, she continues her silence. The star at the end of a run.

I don't know why but I decide to stay behind when Mother goes back to work. Gail Hingley looks in with a tray for Grandma, who glares at me as I carry the food to her bed, then shuts her eyes. I feel hurt, which is insane, all things considered. "There's vegetable soup," I coax, "and a chicken sandwich." Still, nothing. I start munching the sandwich and Grandma opens her eyes. "It's good." I wipe crumbs from my moustache. "The soup's still hot, I'll just…" I stand up and she closes them again. This time I know we aren't playing a game, my spoon the airplane to her mouth, the hangar. "Maybe I could bring Teddy to see you." I hope she can't resist a visit from her great-grandson, who's the only one in the family she can persuade to share tidbits from her plate. "You've got to eat, Grandma. You didn't touch supper last night."

But it's hopeless so I give in, sipping her tea. Part of me belongs here, and I want Grandma to tell me something important, like an eager souvenir hunter on the last day of a holiday, yet she keeps silent. When Gail Hingley returns she smiles at the empty tray and I correct her, embarrassed. "Now about that drink," she falters, working up nerve.

I explain that I'm heading home tomorrow, and the look of disappointment in her eyes makes me sorry.

"I go off duty tonight at . . ."

Ten p.m. After visiting hours, I settle Mother into a taxi and tell her I'm staying on to speak with the Hingleys. She's too tired to object. The air smells of rain, sweet and alive, yet it's clear enough for stars. Since Gail isn't in sight, I take a few deep breaths. Five minutes go by and Hingley drives off in a vast Lincoln. I head back inside, where a furnace blasts enough heat to gag me. I'm sure Gail's forgotten, or perhaps I've misunderstood. We mentioned time, not place.

As I near Grandma's room, Gail comes out and motions me aside. The night nurse will be an hour late so she can't leave yet. I'm ready to call it a day but she rests her hand on my shoulder. Bogart and Bacall, I figure.

"Mm." She tilts her face up toward mine. I notice how she's powdered over the trace of an old acne scar on one side of her cheek. But she has fine blue eyes. Our mouths have a go at it while I survey the hallway for Drooler or one of his pals. Gail presses against me.

The next thing I know, we end up on the spare bed in Grandma's room. Gail pulls a curtain that closes off our private corner, beyond which Grandma snores. We can just about see each other by light from the hall.

"We should save this for later," I whisper, fumbling with the top button on her uniform.

"You know I still live at home," she replies.

"No. I didn't." She starts feeling around my fly, and I have to stop myself from groaning out loud. "Hello, sailor," she teases, her voice soft as possible. "Oh, Gail," I can't hold back, just as something stabs at the curtain.

"Devil! Devil! Who's there?"

Gail shudders, letting go of me.

"Devil!"

I wonder exactly where Grandma is outside the curtain.

"Do something," Gail whispers.

I start humming.

Gail stares like I'm crazy.

"Dum dum de dum, dum de dum de dum dum." *Good night, sweetheart* emerges *Dum dum . . .* Gail joins in my lullaby. *. . . de dum . . .*

"Daddy?" she's crying now. "Is that you?"

There's a crash on the other side of the curtain, and something glass shatters.

"You'd better wait in the lobby," Gail suggests. "I'll calm her down."

I edge away from the bed, staying close to the wall

as Gail goes around the curtain. When she asks "Now what have we here?" I dash for the door.

I pull on my coat, thinking the cameras should have been rolling, but when I hit the lobby something goes off in my head, an overwhelming disgust at the whole human race. All this makes waiting for Gail pointless.

I leave for home the next day after seeing Grandma, my most successful visit if an hour of eye contact counts as success. It bothers me that she may remember last night, or guess I was the Devil, but nothing's said. Grandma will keep my secret. I study her face for the yearning look in her old pictures: bone and hollow defeat me. Yet they seem fitting. When I move to go she clasps my hand tighter. "What, Grandma?" I wait.

Can't you see? her look accuses.

"Grandma?"

"No good," she sighs.

And I try being cheerful, so that I can walk away without smashing Hingley, Gail, Drooler, anyone in sight.

Mike's already developed the film when I get back into town: Grandma stomps, waves her cane, points, yells, cries "Devil!", every image but my own of a silent old lady curled up in her pink flannel nightgown. I think of this a lot, and each night, around seven, imagine Mother heading to the Eldorado. After three days I phone. "I'll bring her home this weekend if she doesn't start eating," Mother says. I don't argue, which amazes both of us.

I'm slashing the script when Mother calls on Saturday afternoon. "Grandma fell," she blurts out. "After lunch. She decided to leave, and got as far as the crosswalk. We don't know what happened."

I piece together that Grandma's in hospital with a broken hip, awaiting surgery to pin the bone.

As soon as we hang up I pack an overnight bag and

make the hour-and-a-half drive home, almost glad it's storming so I have to concentrate on the road. If I start remembering my film about hospitals . . .

Mother and Father wait outside the surgery unit. "This operation can last three hours," she calls, seeing me.

"Grandma's pretty healthy for ninety," I reply.

Barely containing her upset, Mother jabs at a sweater she's knitting. We fill ourselves with coffee and listen to rain outside. After an hour I go for the evening paper.

When I get back, Mother's gasp tells me Grandma hasn't made it through the operation. "It's all my fault," she sobs.

Numb, I put my arm around her.

"I should have quit my job."

Father watches, silent.

"I should have," Mother keeps sobbing.

"I'll miss the old woman," he says finally.

I get through the funeral with some help from Jack Daniel's sour mash. People I should feel connected to show up and stuff themselves with potato salad. Even the Hingleys put in a cameo, though I manage to avoid them. In fact, I avoid whatever I can, a reasonable principle when you think of it. Only once do I insist on my way: I take to the funeral parlour a few daffodils from Grandma's garden—really just unopened buds—and put them into her hand. "Be careful or you'll smear the make-up," says our friendly undertaker, concealing a professional's panic, and with every bit of control in me I reply, "Somehow I don't think she'll mind."

Exit Grandma.

"You should've shot her funeral," Gary says the next time I see him at the station.

"Do you know how much I hate being called 'old buddy'?" I reply.

The thing is, I can't get that dumb song out of my head. I find myself humming while I shower or broil a steak: I keep going back to the tune and, worse, I can't see the footage without it playing along. Actually, it's perfect for the soundtrack, the only one possible. But right now I don't want to go near the show. I've tried sitting through it several times and it's good. Strong lighting, great blocking, every technical feature top-notch. We're up there on the screen, Grandma and Mother and me, and Dad looking his bleakest. If I didn't watch myself I'd break down and cry. After all, it's mine: I made it.

The Album

My parents kept the album in a wooden box that my father had carried through the war in his duffel bag, a box he'd made, with a photograph of Mother glued to the sliding top. Inside, under letters, telegrams, yellowing anniversary cards, a pressed gardenia, lay the album. Even as a child I sensed that it didn't belong in our house.

Ten inches wide, and seven inches high, its cover is of soft canvas printed with tapestry leaves of mossy celadon, the colour of Korea's great pottery, the green of Asia. Although this cloth cover has faded, the black tie holding it together is still taut and looks almost new. The album gives off a musty smell that makes my nose twitch and a dull ache numb my face.

By the time I started school, I'd learned most of the roles life offers from the album's unfamiliar Oriental faces. There I saw the shy scholar, the young couple, the family on holiday, even the old lady alone. I was drawn to the grown-ups more than to the children, a boy biting his lips when the flashbulb frightened him, a little girl in holiday dress, frowning, as she sat on the lap of a visiting relative. Eventually the album acquired a history— Okinawa, the war. But I often wondered (though I never asked) if every family on our block had its own secret mirror from the other side of the globe.

I never expected to return the album.

Father served as a technical sergeant (T-4, or technical fourth grade) in 203rd Port Company, Transportation Corps. His job was operating a ship's winch, loading and unloading ammunition, food, medicine, trucks and sometimes even wounded men. After ten months in Hawaii, during the fall of 1944, the 203rd headed for Okinawa. Though the men didn't know it at the time, they were preparing for the invasion of Japan.

Their ship arrived on the southern coast of an island of stark cliffs, green hills and shot-up trees. Father remembers nothing exotic or beautiful, only weeds, scuffs of grass, dirt, mud. It rained heavily, and the men covered themselves with ponchos before making camp. A few took shelter in an abandoned house surrounded by a garden gone wild. Nearby three goats roamed about, soon coming over to the men, who petted them.

Part of the roof had been blasted away, and rain poured through, soaking torn paper partitions that had been knocked open, leaving one large room. In the corner, on a dirt floor, stood an old mud oven, remains of the cooking area, while thickly woven straw mats covered the rest of the floor. On it, family belongings lay scattered about.

"What kinds of things?" I asked.

"Just old stuff," Father replied. And the eight or ten men who slept inside the house, on the damp mat floor, rummaged through these abandoned treasures, stuffing them into their duffel bags.

"Why did you take the album?"

"I just picked it up. The first thing I could grab."

"What did the other guys take?"

"I don't remember. We were tired, we didn't sit

around comparing."

"Nobody talked about it?"

He shook his head.

Engine trouble delays my flight, leaving several hours to kill in an airport lounge air-conditioned like a deep-freeze. I reach into my overnight bag and take out the album. Questions have always made my father uncomfortable. There's little he can tell me.

Could any neighbour's album have been as fine as ours? One handsome face gives way to another, staring out through a soft patina like bits of life caught in an amber bead. (Father recalls that some of the photographs looked old when he found them.) The black pages resemble heavy ink-blotters, the pictures pasted down in no order that I can detect, except possibly the order in which they were taken; a few are inserted in small paper picture corners. I hold one of these brittle corners and read the faint print across it: IDEAL. There's a design, too, an American eagle, art-deco style. (Did my father use these to put down loose pictures? No, he's assured me.) Beside several of the pictures, inscribed carefully in red ink, are columns of an Asian language I could only recently identify. This writing appears in the first part of the album, where the photographs have yellowed more deeply than the others. (Were the delicate characters written by the family historian? I see a slender old man in black.) Faces appear for a few pages, but not again, although I imagine many resemblances. Near the end is a handful of recent snapshots—recent meaning somewhere between 1930 and 1940. On the back of these, the words "Agfa Tropex" are printed—the name of the film, or of the developer?

Loudspeakers announce "Hong Kong to Okinawa" in

English. By now the lounge is thick with stale cigarette smoke.

Okinawa, I say under my breath. Part of the Ryukyu arc, from the southernmost point of Japan to Formosa. My father's company, the old 203rd, weren't the first Americans to visit there—in 1853, Commodore Perry arrived, and later urged the establishment of an American naval base. But Washington ignored him, and in 1879, Japan took control of the Ryukyus. The native Okinawans, of Chinese origin, were soon reduced to a life of poverty. Prior to the Second World War, the Japanese built airfields on the southern coast, near Naha, the capital, where my flight is headed.

The album begins with two formal portraits of a baby dressed in an ornate silk jacket with a large stiff collar, almost like a figure in an Elizabethan miniature, except for the infant's tight Oriental eyelids. Next, another old studio photograph, of children and women—ten children, including three babies, and eleven women from youth to middle age; inserted in the upper right-hand corner, the portrait of an elderly matriarch. None of these faces turns up again, or none I can identify. Following are several carefully posed studio photographs of a handsome young couple looking directly into the camera, unsmiling but not unhappy. He wears an elaborate dark kimono, she a flowered one, and her embroidered headdress suggests that these must be wedding pictures; both hold unopened fans. Although I can't be certain, there seems to be a resemblance between an older couple who appear later and this stiff proud groom beside his meek bride.

In the following snapshots, most of the men and women wear simple kimonos, and a few have eyeglasses; however, some men are in Western dress, with ties and vests. About halfway through the album, Western clothes predominate—a little girl in a plaid skirt, tights and sandals; a young boy in a sailor shirt, waving a small Japanese flag on a stick. Then, a group photograph of casual young men lined up at a tennis court, with those in the first row sitting crosslegged, and those behind standing against the net. They all hold rackets and wear tennis whites that make me think of *This Side of Paradise*— V-neck sweaters, floppy flannel trousers.

Several snapshots show the house itself, with hills in the distance. There are pots of chrysanthemums set along rock borders, and flowering vines, like clematis, in a garden where wicker chairs have been brought outdoors for a photograph session (the children have their own small wicker chairs). Inside, on a low carved wooden table, you can see a bowl of flowers, and behind it a painted screen with mountains and a waterfall. On the floor, the straw mats Father remembers.

There are also several faint photographs of bridges, men standing beside military trucks and one curious spotted shot of the corner of a fancy carved roof, a bit of barren tree and, on closer look, far off in the empty sky, a small airplane.

Long before Satoko told me, I guessed that this family had come out from Japan to build bridges and other fortifications. The men were engineers, educated, cultured, and the women soft-spoken, gently reserved. All had the easy grace of people who came after conquerors.

During the flight I keep these faces in mind, along with the final words of Satoko's last letter: "Of course you can still return the album by mail, if you prefer." Prefer. Exquisite Oriental politeness? The distance from Hong Kong to Okinawa isn't great.

43

I hadn't given the album a thought while at college, in fact not until the firm of architects I worked for asked me to spend three months on a project in Hong Kong. Even then, I was preoccupied with planning for the trip, and it took the chef at my local sushi bar to make the connection for me. It happened over Kirins. Yoichi was describing a yard sale he'd gone to that afternoon. Piled on a table were some old Japanese prints, poor commercial stuff, and whoever ran the sale explained that her father had brought them back from the war. Suddenly I was telling him about our album. His large knife kept chopping as he described an organization in Japan that collected documents, letters, family mementos, things that had disappeared during the war, and if possible returned them to their owners. He didn't have to say another word. I got the address, photocopied the album and mailed the Xeroxes to Tokyo, eager for a reply. I pictured myself ambling in ancient Zen gardens, arm in arm with a beautiful Japanese girl. For the first time, I wondered if Father had been faithful throughout the war—something else I couldn't ask him.

Shortly before I left for Hong Kong, a letter came, requesting that I send the album directly to Japan. The original family had been found. In a carefully worded reply, I declined. But could I have the address of the original owners? I hadn't yet told my parents of the plan, though I knew they would agree. Returning the album was only just.

Satoko's first letter, from Okinawa, reached me at my Hong Kong office. A distant cousin, working for the organization, had spotted an uncle in one of the Xeroxes, made a few inquiries, and then the discovery.... "You will understand," Satoko explained, "how important it is for us to have the album again."

44

The photographs that trouble me most are the loose ones shoved into the back of the album. A couple in their late fifties entertain their young married son and his wife, and several other grown-up children. At least a dozen photos make up this sequence, the largest. Once, as a boy, I shuffled them like cards in a child's deck of Old Maid, until my father took them away. Married son and mother, son and father, sister alone, wife and sister, husband and wife, two brothers, the parents, all reclining on cushions on the mat floor by the low carved table where, open before them, as if they've been examining it carefully, is our photograph album.

Will Satoko resemble one of these fragile women? Delicate and demure, a latter-day Cio-cio-san? Her back-slanting hand makes me want to hold her letters up to a mirror, in case they have a hidden message. I can't guess her age from the handwriting. If old, how did she spend the war? But surely the eager, self-confident tone of her letters means youth. I imagine her in a pale kimono of spring blossoms, like the wistful young daughter in one of my favourite photographs in the album. She is slowly undoing the silken sash of her robe. I stare out the plane window as we circle over Naha in a green, mouldy sky.

Her eyebrows are full, her lips thin, her hair is parted in the middle, falling into thick waves. She wears an embroidered silk jacket of black, gold and red, designer jeans and the kind of sandals you'd expect on an ex-nun. Though she gives little thought to her appearance, Satoko's face is fresh, alive. I know her at once.

"Did you have a good flight?" She puts out a hand for a firm grip.

"I'm sorry about the delay. Have you been here long?"

45

There was no need for her to meet me at the airport, but she insisted. I half expected the entire family to come out.

"And the album?" She doesn't wait for my answer. "We're so anxious. You must forgive me." She leads me through the lobby, then to an old Buick. "It belongs to my school." She gestures toward the car. "Did you have any problems with customs?"

"Everyone was helpful."

She smiles, opening the car's trunk.

"You speak beautiful English."

"I teach English." She hasn't mentioned that in her letters.

"Do you like poetry? Keats and . . ."

"Oh, no," she laughs. "It's all about falling in love—falling in love and how wonderful it feels. I prefer science fiction." Though we're both around thirty, I feel younger than Satoko, inept.

Satoko leaves me at my hotel, where I shower off the last twenty-four hours. That she might be my teenage dream of Susie Wong seemed entirely within the realm of possibility, but now, as I lather soap over weary muscles, the fantasy embarrasses me.

Satoko's family expects me for tea in an hour, though her invitation made it sound more like a civic occasion. She had already explained that the house in the album was torn down long ago, so I can't see it for my father, or the other guys in the 203rd. Maybe they wouldn't care about the old house, but I don't really believe that. Some nights it must appear in their dreams.

After towelling myself, I thumb through the album one last time. In my filing cabinet at home there's a Xerox copy of it, made for my father. "What would I do with this?" he asked when I gave it to him. "I thought you might want a souvenir." He looked at me like an inscrutable cartoon Chinaman. "Don't you want me to return the album?" Father handed over the Xeroxed pages, saying "I can't remember much about the war."

In the loose photographs at the end of the album, I find my favourite, the delicate young girl I call Asia, and slip it into the pocket of my robe.

Plates of pickled ginger, shredded radish and other foods I don't recognize, arranged in a floral design, are set on the lacquer coffee table, along with scotch, sherry, an ice bucket and Oriental tea bowls. Neither the ceremonial Japanese tea I hoped for, nor an American cocktail party. There is even a bowl of potato chips.

"This is my father," Satoko says, leading me across the room. An elderly man in a well-tailored blazer carefully avoids noticing the large manila envelope under my arm. I notice that he also wears cheap old black shoes. At least eighty, he speaks no English and bows slightly. But his eyes belong to a hanging judge.

"And my brother, Shimamura."

Younger than Satoko, he extends his hand in a frail shake. A teller in the local branch of the Bank of Hong Kong, he recalls one of the album's handsome young tennis players, charming and self-absorbed.

"My aunt and uncle are unable to join us," Satoko continues. "Would you like a cocktail? Or some tea?" Disappointed, I suggest tea. No crowd, no tearful reunion. My imperialism must be unbounded.

"How did you find Hong Kong?" Shimamura asks, and I sense that he would prefer scotch, although clearly we will all have tea.

Satoko disappears into the kitchen; we might be in

47

any Michigan Avenue highrise.

"A little hectic. This is my first visit—my firm has an office there."

He nods, as their father quietly sits, folding his hands. "I don't like Hong Kong," Shimamura observes, smiling. "It's too noisy."

Would they be relieved to know that Father's honourable discharge reads, "Asiatic-Pacific ribbon, 2 bronze stars; Philippine liberation ribbon, 1 bronze star; good-conduct ribbon; victory medal"? I could emphasize the good-conduct ribbon. Satoko returns, glaring at her brother. "Do you like it?" she asks me.

"Well, I haven't seen much yet. But I stayed in the Mandarin, which is very beautiful."

"My father stayed there once," she replies. "Some years ago."

I take the envelope from my lap and hand it to Satoko, but before she can reach for it, I stop, holding the parcel in mid-air. Turning toward her father, I lean forward and present it to him. He nods again, and sets it in his lap for several seconds. None of us breathes as he opens the flap and pulls out the album.

"I didn't want to mail it. And since I was going to be in Hong Kong anyway. . . ."

The old man opens the album, and stares at the first photograph. I know the face that looks back at him. He keeps staring, expressionless, without turning the page.

"Why have you come?" asks Shimamura.

Satoko interrupts firmly in Japanese.

I sit there, heartsick. I have given away our family album.

After School

i

The time of day is after school, that hour before the father comes home, intrudes himself on the house, the wife, the boy. This hour belongs to a slant of late-afternoon light, water splashing on vegetables in the kitchen sink, bustle before dinner, which ruins it all: he will be there too.

Stop. Think that this time can go on and on. She plunges—almost with glee—her hands into the mixture of ground meat and breadcrumbs and onions, which he helped chop, and squishes it together (he listens to the egg mixing in, fascinated) and he watches her face, her expression, because she knows how to mix it just right. The way they like it. He—the father—will probably say something like "Meatloaf again?" and the boy, of course, can't know that on the money she has for shopping, the money he gives her, meatloaf is battleground. No, what he sees is that she is hurt, the hour they've spent together somehow attacked by that swift, casual "Meatloaf again?" Does he not appreciate the sound of squishing egg? Can't he imagine it, even?

Better not, or he'd want to be there, and ruin that hour too. But it is theirs. From the minute he runs in the house and announces that on today's spelling test he scored one hundred, and she kisses his cheek, and offers a chocolate-chip cookie and milk, and pushes her bangs to one side of her face, adding "Two cookies today, because you spell so good," they feel a thrill of conspiracy, as if scoring one hundred proves he will grow up and take care of her some day, all by himself. Days ahead when he will score so many one hundreds for her.

But nothing is this simple, he knows, already. Without *him* ruining the hour, it can explode, or fall to someone else, a telephone caller, an aunt with news, a neighbour with gossip. Or, worse, she might simply tell him to go out and play—the worst of all fates, because there is no point in settling down in a kitchen chair near the stove and waiting for her phone call to end. "Why don't you go outside for a while?" This she might say with a special lilt, as if he'd want to, which of course is a betrayal, for she should know better. Or she might say it hurriedly, and then he knows she will have on a different dress when he comes back inside, and there will be fresh powder on her cheeks, and she won't want him to muss her. Maybe they will go out that evening—for now she joins *him* to become a they—or maybe they won't. No matter, the hour is lost.

An hour can get lost this way, an hour is a fragile thing; an hour is frightening.

It might not happen, though. Most days she will be alone, the telephone won't ring, milk and cookies await him along with a hug and smile that tells how she's missed him since lunch. He might read to her from a library book while she starts dinner, stumbling over new big words, or she might read to him if dinner is "under control." He likes reading to her best. She is a good audience, smiling when he gets it right, patient as he sounds out an unfamiliar name. And all the while peeling, chopping, mixing, as if she has special powers and chooses not to call upon them with a snap of her fingers, because that would be like neighbour ladies who take frozen packages from the refrigerator and just heat them up. His mother would never do that.

Best are the days when she is "running a little late" with dessert. There might be a bowl of icing to lick clean, or beaters with a few globs of whipped cream sticking to them. (He likes chocolate best.) She loves making fancy sweet things, and he takes special pride in these. Whenever people come for Sunday dinner, everyone makes a fuss about her desserts, the desserts he has watched her make so many afternoons: measure out flour, sugar, butter; sift and measure and sift; measure cream or vanilla (ah, vanilla—she lets him sniff the wonderful bottle for a moment, before capping it). Always she knows exactly how much of everything to put in, and though he doesn't know, exactly, it becomes their secret. *He* never watches her do this. "Yes, my wife likes baking," *he* might say.

Better still to sit at the kitchen table, elbows propped carefully ("Remember, don't move, don't shake the table"), while she smooths on icing, her knife making small whirls, circles of sugar, delicate peaks, as she surveys the creation, biting her lip while perhaps deciding on a border of piped cream or shaved nuts, or sliced cherries or strawberries, in summer. Endless possibilities. Then she stands back and smiles, offering him the spoon to lick, a reward for not shaking the table, and while she fills the sink with dishes, and starts running water, he opens a book and they move into the world of dogs and cats and horses and such happiness: her reward.

If there is time she might say "Now let's go into the living room" and he will run ahead to turn on the lamp, lighting up blotches of wallpaper flowers the colour of old

51

dried blood; and she follows in a minute or two, having stopped to pat down her hair, or run a comb through it. Now the waiting begins, their hour coming to an end, and he asks about her afternoon, giving the mother back to that world of grown-ups. This is the time when she might tell of a trip to the market and bring out a surprise, a new colouring book, an eraser shaped like a frog. She is sorry to be giving him up, too. They wait together. The end of an hour can be terrible.

But sometimes when he runs in the back door she will say "yes" from a great distance. Not exactly startled, yet not expecting him, either, she comes out from the pantry to kiss him, with the far-away look in her eyes, the strong smell on her breath, like that stuff he's seen his father pour into ginger ale. Maybe she'll burn the roast, for there are usually roasts on such days—then slamming dishes and tears. No reading, no stories, no watching her peel carrots, but a look that makes him close up, as if he has brought the cold March persistence inside with him. And oh, how he wanted to tell about a girl who threw up in class and everyone giggled and held their noses, and the janitor had to come in and sprinkle sawdust on "it" while their teacher said "Stay in your seats, please." He did, hating the first-grade room with a passion. He looked at the clock: the big hand on twelve, the little hand on three. Soon he would be home, to tell her all about it.

Why didn't she want to hear?

"Play in your room," she said.

He went to his room. He had done nothing wrong. He would not cry.

At first he sat very still on his bed, without turning on a light, as if darkness might hold him up. Then his heels began kicking rhythmically against one side of the mattress. He kicked this way until realizing the bedspread would get dirty. There were books to look at, toys to hold, paper and crayons, but he didn't want any of them. After sitting a while longer, he tiptoed downstairs, back into the kitchen. He knew she would be in the pantry, climbed onto one of the kitchen chairs and sat with folded hands. An uncovered pot of water boiled furiously, steaming the kitchen window behind the stove. "I'm sorry," he said.

She came out, possibly humming. "I forgot to peel the potatoes. We'll have mashed potatoes."

"Someone threw up in class today."

"Oh."

Water splashed in the sink.

He watched her hands move, scraping, peeling. She had on her polka-dot apron with the red bow, but hadn't tied it in back. He climbed down and stepped behind her; she kept on peeling. He decided to reach for the ties and make a bow, the way he tied his shoelaces. Then he heard a car in the drive, and the hour was over. He opened his mouth and leaned forward and bit her, hard, on the behind.

ii

The boy wanted a surprise. Every day now he wanted one.

Last fall his mother had promised a new baby—a brother, or sister. After talking about this for several months, she took sick, was put in hospital and—like that!—no more talk of "baby." He felt tricked, then ashamed: he shouldn't get excited about a baby, he was too old for that. "Don't be sad," his father had said as they left the hospital from visiting. "After all, you're a big boy." Six, and a big boy. Then his jacket zipper stuck. The father knelt down to pull, twist, loosen it, and the boy didn't know why he felt like crying. "I can fix it," he mumbled, angry. "Just stand still now." Was his father angry too?

The boy didn't want to think about "baby" as he ambled home, stopping before the window display of his favourite variety store. But today he remembered, for the first time in months, because his teacher had worn a strange loose dress to class and several kids had whispered "She's pregnant." His mother never looked so fat. Maybe she hadn't been pregnant; maybe she lied. He didn't like to think that and walked faster, carefully stepping on each block of sidewalk to avoid the cracks, half humming a schoolyard chant: *Don't step on a crack, or you'll break your mother's back.* Part of him believed it. He stopped, foot in air, ready to come down smack on the concrete, lowered it, almost touched ground, before lurching forward to avoid the cement seam.

At the corner of his street, the boy slackened a bit. There was nowhere to go but home. He passed the corner house, with six left. One, two . . . He stopped to look up at a tree. The sky had clouded over since lunchtime. Three, four, five . . . Could there be a nice surprise?

In the front hallway, a suitcase.

The boy's stomach jumped.

"I'm leaving. I can't stay here any longer." His mother sat tensely on the sofa, her coat unbuttoned. She fingered a plaid wool scarf. "But I wanted to say good-bye."

"Mama!" he cried out.

"I have to go." She looked at her scarf, for some reason annoyed with it, and then stuffed the thing into her pocket.

"Don't, Mama." He ran over to her side.

"You're too young to understand."

"Mama!"

Eyes vacant, she stood up as he grabbed onto her arm.

"No."

She stepped forward.

"You can't."

"Tell your father I've gone."

"Mama please!" His father would say, keep her calm.

She crossed the rug even though he pulled her back.

"Talk to me, Mama."

"I have to go. Some day you'll understand. It's better . . ."

"No!"

"Don't," she yelled. "You're twisting my arm."

He could hardly breathe, and began choking.

She pulled away, ran into the hall and picked up her suitcase.

For an instant he stood still, not moving, or not able to move. Then he ran after her, but by now she'd opened the front door and was stepping out, onto the porch.

"Don't make a fuss," she said. Pursed lips.

He reached for the suitcase but she clutched it to her side.

"Not in front of the neighbours. With everyone watching."

"Can I come with you?"

"No." She went down the steps. "I don't know where I'm going."

He followed.

"Don't," she said.

A moment's hesitation. His eyes filled with tears.

"Please."

She took the scarf from her pocket and tied it about her neck. Then she put her hand back into the coat pocket, searching, and sighed, "I don't have my gloves."

He stared at her, hoping she would go back in the house, where he could try harder.

"Never mind. I'll buy new ones. I never much liked those anyway. Your father gave them to me." She headed down the front walk and up the street, toward the boulevard where, he knew, there would be buses and taxis and the start of far-off places.

"Come home, Mama."

"You don't understand." She continued walking.

"I do too."

"You couldn't possibly." The exasperation in her voice cut him off, and they walked side by side, silently. Lights began to come on in some of the houses.

"I'll be good," he burst out. "If only . . ."

She looked at him, despairing. "It's not you. It's never you. I just don't belong."

Her words touched safety. When she talked about not belonging it usually meant they would soon turn around and go home; they wouldn't even get as far as the boulevard, the bus stop—that panic.

Then he smiled a little. "It's starting to rain."

Both of them looked up, and a few cold drops hit their faces. She smiled too—grateful perhaps, with an expression of comfort—and said, "Well, I don't have my umbrella. I hate to buy gloves *and* an umbrella."

Now they watched each other; it was over.

As they turned around, and headed back home, he didn't think about the times this had happened before, or the times it might happen again. "Can I carry the suitcase?" he asked.

She gave it up. As he lifted the suitcase from her hand she felt its weight vanish into him, making the boy smile again because this time, as usual, it was empty.

iii

He'd been carrying the picture in his pocket for several days, anxious to welcome her home with a present. Ready now, he sat on the front steps. She would probably wave as soon as the car turned into their drive. Then he'd wave back and run over to kiss her and give his surprise. Third from the left, in the front row, he'd held a smile until the flashbulb went off. Not one of the taller boys, but not the shortest, either. She'll spot me right away, he felt certain, when the photos were passed out during recess. Better, though, were the wallet-sized pictures where he stood by himself in a sweater with reindeer prancing across his chest. He knew she would be glad he remembered to wear it. "I want your picture just like this," she said the first time he pulled on the sweater. *Hilliard Elementary School, grade two*—he read the words printed beneath his picture with growing excitement.

Since she went into hospital he had a lot to remember. Each morning his father left a glass of orange juice on the sink, but nothing else. He had to make his own breakfast, wash up the dishes, pack a sandwich for lunch, brush his teeth before leaving the house. And check to be sure he locked the door behind himself. All this because she couldn't be there.

Eight long weeks. At first he counted off days, but then he stopped. "She needs this rest," his father explained once while tucking him in. And another time, "She's still resting. Maybe we can visit next Sunday." But they never did. He didn't see why his father wouldn't talk abut her, so it must be bad. It must be even worse than bad, because his father let him do things she never allowed: for supper they ate drive-in hamburgers or take-out Chinese; sometimes he wore the same socks two days in a row; and after school he could watch cartoons on TV until dinner. Even then they left the set running. "Pretend we're on vacation," his father suggested, though it didn't feel like that.

"When will she get enough rest?" he wanted to know. Often he imagined her walking toward him with arms out, ready for a big hug. "Pretty soon. We've got to be patient."

But he didn't like patience. Anyway, he wouldn't need it after tonight. They could be happy instead. They would "go out for dinner," which meant somewhere with a fancy tablecloth and maybe candles. She would like that, so he would too. He would sit up straight and listen because she must be very tired. He knew how to make her happy. Already he'd picked some tulips from Mrs. Wyckoff's garden next door and put them in his mother's favourite vase. Mrs. Wyckoff had also cut lilac from branches he couldn't reach and added these to the bouquet. She liked to give things. Since his mother went away, Mrs. Wyckoff made him cookies every Saturday, and if his father worked late, read stories out loud as he snuggled against her.

When the pictures came he set one aside for Mrs. Wyckoff. "You'll break all the girls' hearts some day," she said, putting it in the photo-section of her wallet. "These are my grandchildren." She showed him faces of a boy and girl about his own age. "They live far away. In California." He gave a big grin. "You can have another picture," he offered. Smiling, she shook her head. "Just wait till your mother sees how you've grown."

This made him worry. At home he went into the

bathroom and compared his face in the mirror with a school photo. Except for last week's haircut he looked the same. He wanted things to be like before. Some nights she used to stand outside his bedroom watching him pretend sleep, and if he didn't move she stood there longer. Maybe she had changed too. Maybe she wouldn't want to stand there, just watching, glass in hand. He remembered how the ice cubes cracked against each other when she sipped.

As if it could bring her faster, he ran across the grass, looking both ways. They usually drove home from the right, but he wasn't taking any chances.

A few cars passed. Suddenly he wondered if Mrs. Wyckoff stood in her living-room window. He turned around, startled that she did. He hated it but waved. Why didn't they come? He put a hand in his pocket to touch the picture. Safe.

Before she went away there had been a big fight, on his birthday. All afternoon he'd watched the clock at school, eager for supper and presents and one of her chocolate cakes. He would blow out every candle and make them light the cake again so he could get two wishes. She had agreed at breakfast.

"How could you?" his father yelled as he ran into the house.

Why wasn't he still at work?

"Don't," said Mrs. Wyckoff, who shouldn't be there either.

His mother lay on the floor in front of the sofa.

"She'll be fine," Mrs. Wyckoff explained, hurrying over once she spotted him.

"Mama!" He pushed by. Her eyes stared at the ceiling.

An ambulance came and men carried her out on a stretcher, like TV doctors.

He forgot his birthday until much later that night, when his father brought out presents. "I don't want them," he cried.

Eight long weeks. He hated remembering and went to the steps again, where he took out his photo: it had to make her happy. And he'd done everything else right. Like magic they drove up before he saw to wave. The motor stopped by the garage in back so he couldn't watch her climb out. But voices, laughter, talking, he heard it all. Mrs. Wyckoff hurried to say "hello" over the fence. Her dog barked.

Someone called his name but he kept staring ahead at the street. More laughter, more barking. Soon everyone in the neighbourhood heard them.

But he would never go back there to hug her. He wouldn't take her the picture, either. No, he would not.

Some of the Old Good Feelings

People think what they want—if there's one thing I've learned, that's about it. Which is not much to say for seventy-five years. I don't want to remember most of the time; usually I can fight off memories. Human, we tell ourselves. To help pass time I pour another bourbon, put on one of my old records, maybe with Jane Wylie singing and Duff Gere on the sax, the mellow sound of them together—the two of them off and on for ten years of making up, until she finally mixed enough pills and vodka in their suite at the Drake, long after we stopped playing Chicago—and I can almost block out the years since.

There was even a Thanksgiving I spent in bed with Jane, after one of her fights with Duff. I think she cried as I touched her breasts. I'm sure of it, and when I joked, "Were your nipples always so prominent?" she answered, half grimly, "Years of abuse." I don't remember what we ate. Some kind of room-service food. And later that night, back in my own room, showering, I saw I had crabs, and thought to myself, "Won't Duff have a surprise in store for him." I never much liked Duff, so I didn't tell Jane, who could have picked them up from any number of guys. Crabs: the price of a sex life. The price of being human.

One thing I hate is when record companies phone up about turning my 78s into stereo albums called "classic" or "the best of" or "favourites." Maybe I should be proud: Nick Collins and his Orchestra. The best hotels. The Waldorf-Astoria, the Ritz. Played them all. White linen tablecloths, heavy silver, sparkling cocktail shakers, Manhattans with breakfast. "The war-time sound." What the hell is that supposed to mean to me now? *Night and day, you are the one.* Nice, as sentiment goes. Why not?

Funny things you remember, too: one fine black hair growing beside Jane's nipple, but I can't recall which, left or right. Anyway, we got a kick out of each other that Thanksgiving. How many years ago? Thirty-seven, at least. And I never guessed then I'd live long enough to end up reminiscing over a dead woman's nipple.

Musical memories all you bargained for?

This isn't what you expected?

If I'm going to talk into a damn machine, if I'm going to put it down for you, then sonny, you don't get to dictate. You'd be here if I wanted that. All of you alike, the same eager face, wanting a special tidbit, the same lanky-haired girlfriend lugging your tape recorder. What a laugh. Do you think I earned my reputation playing for the likes of you?

I played at the Plaza, remember. No other Canadian played there.

And I ended up back home, after all, because the big bands lasted a decade longer here. The Palace Pier, the CNE, Banff. We kept on playing after our time, and today you dare call me "classic." Once I read myself described as a "legend."

Coughing. A switch clicks off, then on again.

Emphysema. But you know that already, it's part of the "official" biography—newspaper clippings, whatever. You did your homework? I don't care.

Right now I care for Jane Wylie's nipples. Cinnamon, they were. Poor Jane.

There are people alive all over the world, your own special ones, and something like a thread holds you to them. The dead, too. What I see outside my window has nothing to do with this: white ash bark, red leaves, brown ones. My own half-acre. Thick and private. Like . . . I can still think about sex. I can remember.

Denny ran ahead of me through the trees. October then, too, somewhere in Vermont, a morning's drive from Boston. How far back—'43? Early October, because warm. Hot. He ran ahead, slapping a long twig against the bushes we passed, making leaves rustle, turning the colours, and then he stopped and looked at me, laughing. He knew how beautiful he was.

Remember, he played solo clarinet in Jane's ballads, and doubled on alto sax. His lips a bit too thick, sensuous.

Walking slow, Denny took off his shirt and tied it around his waist, sleeves dangling below his belt buckle as the sun followed him. Then he ran on, slapping bushes with another branch, enjoying my admiration. A kid, to me. Twelve years younger. Just a kid, full of his power.

That night I touched him so many places. Over and over.

You didn't know? It's not part of the "official" blurb?

What am I, you're thinking—a nasty old man remembering every warm hole?

Don't make me laugh. Denny was beautiful.

Of all the men my mind goes back to Denny. And Jane, who never belonged to me, is the woman. Odd. Because if you name a place, say Atlantic City, it conjures a body. A body on a bed. Hotels don't do that, they're too impersonal even after you get to know them. The same

63

room, six months later, still has had too much taking place for any sense of home. Cities are different. I've felt at home in cities. Sure I had a flat where I left my onyx brushes, old photographs, stuff you don't carry on the road. The cocktail shaker from Harrods, a Christmas present one year from Jane and Duff. That sort of thing. But I never felt home there, not really, without a body on the bed.

Meals out late.

Alone a lot.

Now this place is too quiet—no Mac bumping into furniture. A dead dog. How can I say "my last companion" without a note of self-pity? I don't mean that.

Denny buried his face in my stomach, laughing all the while, and I held his neck hard. We clung together. Later on, in the rehearsal hall, he'd spend hours with Duff and Paul Stein working to match the speed of their vibrato—a characteristic of our sound, you remember.

Five months like that. Loving talk, pretty tokens—all of it. Over breakfast, a hand on mine. With so many plans.

Then he went off saying we'd be friends, as if nothing had happened.

Jane guessed. This must have been ten years before she killed herself. Probably noticed me watching Denny during rehearsals. I never could cover up what I felt.

Jane Wylie: Jeannette-Marie Wylie, a French Canadian mother and a shanty-Irish old man. We had a bond as ex-Montrealers, Jane and me. Imagine her at eighteen. No one had caressed that young body. Sweet, new. We used to play a song that went, *What is love, but the kisses you give and take?*

I have too many threads with dead people. Jane,

there were nights I would have held you with such patience, no one ever guessed it of me. Perhaps the hotel was full of couples promising each other "I only want to make you happy." Maybe it matters that for a while they felt it.

The afternoon Denny left, Jane sat on the foot of my bed, wearing one of those dresses with padded shoulders, a silky grey thing, and said, "You'll be okay, Nick."

I must have been pouring drinks.

"He's trouble, can't you see? It's only charm, he uses it on everyone to charm himself. But he doesn't believe it in the end."

I got angry then. "Just because we've been to bed doesn't give you any right to talk like that."

"Okay. Sorry." She swung her foot back and forth and I remember watching it. Expensive new evening shoes, silver, with fancy thin straps. "But he's everybody's Denny. He wants everybody."

Maybe I told her to get out, I don't remember what happened next. She didn't leave, though, she kept sitting there, swinging one foot, looking down occasionally to admire her shoes. Finally I suggested we get some dinner and she stared up at me, half smiling, but sort of sad, and confessed, "I can't walk anywhere far in these."

We both stood there laughing, yet I wanted Denny so badly. A body presses itself into your mind like that.

Jane and I were decent to each other, but we never ended up in bed again.

She took my favourite tune from Al Bowlly. *Maybe it's because I love you too much,* she'd sing, and everyone's eyes would cloud over. *Maybe that is why you love me so little. Maybe when I answered yes . . .* How do the lyrics go? *Maybe I become a bore . . .* Anyway, it doesn't last. What no one talks about is the contradiction.

Of course we knew. Lyrics going one way but the rhythm, the upbeat, the music, another. We didn't have time for all those emotions. Listen to my recording of "Midnight, the stars and you." Just listen.

They say sex can come from friendship. Okay. Whenever I tried, it didn't last. Bodies don't blur together; some I forget, but that's different. Wouldn't want to remember them all. An upper berth, a young soldier, a bad hand job while I looked out the window at blue lights flashing by. The marks where a girl's bra cut into her back, my tongue on them. These aren't blurs. At the time you know they're not for remembering. I learned after a while.

Some nice girls, real nice ones, but Duff always joked, "What are you doing with her? She's not like the usual trash." I never thought to marry. The others did—a bandleader and his wife, common newspaper picture. Always nice girls. A conventional lot, bandleaders, though they played around plenty on the road. I won't tell names, sonny, so relax, here's another disappointment. Don't push your nostalgia at me. I lived then, goddamn it. I need more bourbon.

A switch clicks the tape off and then on again.

I remember thinking once how I'd never let myself become an old man. Not really old. One of those guys you see on the street, bent over a cane, dressed for the weather. Watching his steps. Sixty hits, and limp erections. Never had much trouble, though some guys do. Always stamina. Maybe that's why I never thought to marry.

But I might've married Jane if Duff had died first. That nice heart attack sooner. Ifs. He outlived her only five years, dropped dead at a Chicago Athletic Club. Wonder what he thought, finding her body passed out one more time, yet that time for good.

Went to Jane's funeral. March 11, 1955. Two days before I turned fifty. Easy to remember. A week's drunk, then. Chrysanthemums, gladioli, roses, all those flowers for a pretty Montreal girl smeared with middle age and booze. Her hair had thinned, I noticed—open coffin, incredible! For Duff. Sonofabitch. Goddamn sonofabitch.

Jane, old with me. Picture it. Sweaters and fruit juice and tea. Domestic. Spike the tea. Iced tea, half vodka, that's how we drank it in summer.

Instead, alone. A long time. Watch TV. Never read. Other night watched a program about "gays"— they've got a name. Not when I did it. Not with Denny. Or the others. And all my women, well . . . at least no one's found a new word for that.

A lot of things don't have words. That's something else I know. Like what I did to Mac this morning. For Mac? For me? Stupid old blind dog. A problem with collies, long about five years some of them start going blind. Bad blood. Whatever. Had other dogs before, in the last fifteen years. Never wanted one when I was younger. Pets. Hell, the world had too many people in it for me to want a pet. Then one day, for my sixtieth birthday, I thought, it's time to make a home. So I bought the first Mac. Called them all that, no matter what breed. One retriever—stupid—and a shepherd, before Mac.

I took him out in the woods, let him lick my hand, waited for him to curl up in the leaves, aimed my rifle, knew it was right, and shot him in the side of his head. Couldn't let a vet do it. Murder? You'll understand, if you get old.

I know, this isn't what you want. Better an ageing Fred Astaire type. Smooth, polished. I didn't age well, my features coarsened. But then, what I wanted was my life alone. How much does anyone care?

Passion is logical. Sex is logical; the body knows. Last time I had a body on this bed, I was sixty-five. Ten years ago. Sometimes use my hand now, but not often. I knew sex. Closed that door.

Ten years.

Click off, click on. Music in background.

Jane, Denny, stay with me.

Let it go!

I'll tell you this. I'll tell you. Life is an old man's cock—if you play around with it long enough, you're bound to get something out of it.

Too nasty? Sonny, where I'm going. . . .

Remember, I took care of myself. And well.

Sometimes I rant at both of you, maybe that's stupid for me to admit now. All sorts of talks I've had with you, inside me. Ifs. You don't want to know. I don't blame you.

Into the sauce.

What's around? Turn on the TV, the radio. Music today is nothing. In the last twenty years, maybe five melodies worth playing. *Your eyes are the eyes of a woman in love.* That's one. How we'd have played it. Couples swaying, poor little secretaries dolled up for their night on the pier, feeling magic, the magic we gave them, *Your eyes . . .* floating out over the water, dark, moon ripples. Mine.

You can hear it now, for the price of an album, but no one can smell it, feel it, not those nights.

When I stopped hearing it we split up. Eras end. We knew it. Lucky, I'd made money, never much good with it, still I had enough. And the old Montreal house, my parents'. Him, a banker, with the bandleader son. Hot shot. Neither of them lived past seventy.

There's more. And plenty bourbon. Lugged it

myself. Saw myself. In Dominion's window. An old man, dressed for all weather, lugging his bag from the liquor store. Get that: lugging. No cane. I stood there, pulled myself up and watched that reflection. It coughed, started choking. Wiped its mouth. Me? Why not.

Let it go!

We shared a past.

Someone dies first. My mother, pneumonia, my father, cancer. Jane chose. Others along the way. Jane not there to help that morning I got up, went downstairs for breakfast, felt a bad omen, stopped in the newsstand. Denny's face on the front page.

DENNY WRIGHT IN CRASH

I bought the paper: June 22, 1960. You hadn't turned forty. Out driving, drinking, always reckless, booze, drugs, men, women. Alone.

Everyone called it an accident, but I knew better. You went like Jane did.

A cathedral funeral, so many loved you. Didn't go. What for?

Should have.

Loved you.

Such thighs. Still remember. Your face buried in my stomach. A charmer, Jane said. You wouldn't let me help.

Last time we met, years after Boston, I couldn't remember your body. Sitting together, a bar somewhere, some city, I felt your looks, still little boy wounded. Now thirty-five. Did I have those too? Once. They used to call me vulnerable. Ha! I watched you raise your glass, a straight-up martini, and one thing came clear. All that charm meant nothing to you. Jane had been right. I felt old for the first time. What was I? And I thought to myself, Nick Collins, this is when you start getting old. Too young

for such thoughts. Drunk all weekend. Plenty of sex.
Every night, sometimes, new arms, legs, bellies. They
don't blur.

Liar.

What I wanted was. . .

Spit it out.

. . . love?

No.

No.

"But I love you, Nick. Doesn't that matter?" I've
heard those words more than once.

Pitiful. We're all pitiful: Here, I bring you my
need. Goddamn it. Need me.

Sex dies. We'll be friends. See you sometime for
drinks. In time we'll be friends. I'm a good friend, you
know.

This morning I wanted that clipping, the one of
Denny. Crazy, but all these years I've saved it. Never
saved Jane's. Don't remember reading one. Duff called,
crying: "You'll come out? Jane always loved you." Sure
I went. How else could I see him destroyed?

Looked through drawers, piles of paper, too much
paper. Nowhere around. It doesn't matter.

Goddamn it. I can see that funny crooked smile.

Jane held me, put her arms around me, the day you
left. Someone knew.

You should have gone to bed with me again. Not
to was wrong. And I should have gone to bed again with
Jane. Maybe sex didn't die, maybe we killed it.

Both of you had that same crooked smile.

No good pictures here, though we're all in *The Big
Bands*. I found each of us today. Names identified, dates
given, gigs listed—for what? Somebody to look up. It's
not music. But I looked us up. Jane wearing orchids.

White ones, with dark purple centres. Of course the picture's black and white, but Jane seldom wore orchids, and only white ones, after she and Duff fought. "Why does he buy them?" she once asked me. His notion of what a lady wants, I guessed. Did she shrug?

I'll give Duff this—he stayed. Others would have walked out. At the first scent of a problem I turned. Always a reason. Good ones, too. Duff stayed. Old sonofabitch. But Jane was special. We all were, in our way. A charming lot.

They go together, you know, charm and suicide. They're one.

Goddamn.

I'm responsible. I took the dog into the woods and shot him. Didn't ask anyone's help. Didn't leave him behind for someone else to look after. Who wants an old blind dog? For the pound to kill. I took care of my own.

Now do you see? I'm not waiting around for the cane.

Plenty bourbon tonight. Play the old songs. Oh I had times. Goddamn. Jane, Denny, who else but you now? Shoulders, bellies and scotch. What did we know? The middle of the night, hangover heads, laughter. Manhattans with breakfast. Shoulders and bellies. Some moments of tenderness. Later on, angry words. That joy of undressing for the first time. Back to music again. Needing someone. A body on the bed. Music. A body. And I knew something about love, I knew. . . .

End of tape.

Coroner's Inquest:
Collins, Nicholas W.
Exhibit no. 3

Not in China

I had no intention of causing trouble, but it came along anyway. In fact, I'll even admit a little satisfaction that there was never a plan, a conscious decision on my part. Some things just happen this way—isn't that what's meant by chance? You get taken over by it.

Of course I knew all the regular churches: St. Mary's Anglican, which sounds like you're sitting in the bottom of a well; the Grace United, nice and clear; St. Paul's, with its cotton-batting air; and the good old brick Lutheran. Still, church gigs are the pits, even though the best pick-up ensembles—like Old Musick, or the Bach Chamber Choir—use as many symphony members as possible. An honour, of sorts. So I agree, fully aware I'm walking into prima donnas, crummy acoustics and poor rehearsal time. But you can get used to almost anything for love. Until two months ago, whenever I accepted a church gig, I had only my career in mind.

Mira is beautiful. Tall, strong-boned, with thick blonde hair. She manages to look dignified playing the cello, no small accomplishment for a woman. Sometimes she even resembles a primitive stone carving, an earth mother. When I told her this Mira choked with laughter. "What else do you expect from a Czech peasant?" Twice a year Mira makes up a secret potion from her great-grandmother's recipe, weird herbs and oils, which she sells to other girls in her section. A few of them insist it works, but I haven't seen much evidence on their skin. Mira's complexion, however, is silk.

I've heard enough comments about her from guys in my section (woodwinds, I'm first oboe) to know that Mira can have her pick of the orchestra, but beauty is only part of her power. She's also an extraordinary cellist, really musical, and not just a technician who makes sound overflow without the least bit of meaning. I'll never forget the time I heard her practising a particularly sad melody from Brahms, its line spun out until all the world's longing converged in Mira's bow. Perhaps that was the moment I became hers.

Not the orchestra's first Tristan and Isolde, we were still careful. Anyway, an aura of secrecy is part of Mira's style. She fled Czechoslovakia with her husband, Josef, after the Russians invaded in '68, and within two years Josef established an export business and purchased his first Mercedes. Only one subject of conversation interested him: diatribes against Communism. To hear Josef tell it, there are no social problems in Canada, no injustices of consequence. My wife, Pat, who treats disturbed children with music therapy, is far more sympathetic, but she hasn't changed since we met as conservatory students.

Both Josef and Pat remained home with responsibilities when Mira and I first locked hands on the Great Wall. This, during our orchestra's much-publicized China tour. Until that moment, only our eyes had revealed what both of us guessed was becoming inevitable. So there we stood, lost among a hundred other musicians with assorted cameras, all busy snapping at that bleak cold air, which makes a sort of awesome beauty "if you like scenery," as Mira whispered.

"Don't you?" I was sure we'd agree.

"If I have to see one more factory of lacquer vases, one more Maoist dance class, one more . . ."

We both laughed now.

"Do I detect Chairman Mao hasn't won your heart?"

Before she could answer, the principal flute, who is my best friend, appeared waving his Polaroid. "Come on, don't you want your pictures taken on the Great Wall?"

"Just what I always wanted, Barry."

"Well get closer, you two. Christ, put your arm around her, Tim." Had he guessed?

The Polaroid did its job and in less than a minute Barry handed us the souvenir. "Now one for Mira."

"I never save photographs," she apologized. "But thanks." Mira drew away to wander along the wall.

"Something wrong?" Barry asked.

I shrugged.

"Maybe she's missing Josef," he joked, hurrying off for a few more shots before we were herded back to the tourist bus.

I went after Mira but she'd fallen in with a group of fiddle players. Then someone called to us, probably one of the Chinese translators, whose voice disappeared in the vast space. Like our tour guide, with eyes swathed in deliberate emptiness, Mira turned and headed toward the bus. I surveyed the landscape one last time, already feeling a pleasant nostalgia for the barren old hills and cold wind.

I didn't speak to Mira alone until the next morning, and this was hardly a private talk. Down one of Peking's side streets, really an alley in the city's oldest section, several of us headed with our translator to a shop specializing in Chinese folk instruments. Mira was already there when we entered, along with half a dozen other orchestra members. The tiny shop, dark and stuffy, had a stove glowing in the middle of the room. One of our translators kept all the local Chinese outside, but they peered in at us, noses against the window.

Mira seemed in her element. Though the shop was chilly, she'd slipped off her sheepskin coat and sat on a bench near the stove, with one of those old Chinese men who look ageless. She held a one-stringed instrument that he helped her play. An erhu, I later learned its name. The instrument's base rested upright on her knee, and she held it like a cello, with her right hand on a bow that somehow connected to the erhu. The old man shaped her hand over the stick, which she now held underhand. "Just like a viola da gamba bow," Mira exclaimed, and then she made a dreadful whiny sound with the instrument. "We're lucky it doesn't have much volume," Barry remarked under his breath. Mira kept sawing away at this eerie wail, causing titters from the shopkeeper and laughter from everyone else.

Never in my life have I longed for a woman as much as I wanted Mira at that moment.

Finally she stopped sawing and said a few words to one of the translators, who related them in Chinese to the shopkeeper—obviously a business transaction that left everyone pleased, and Mira the proud owner of an erhu.

I went over. "What'll you do with it back home?"

"Hang it on the wall in my studio." She held the thing almost protectively. "That way everyone who drops by will see I've been to China."

We both stared down at the erhu just as one of the

guys in my section began blowing shrieks on a double-reed instrument.

"I want to be in bed with you." I felt sure no one could hear.

Mira smiled, that warm, wide smile which makes my knees shake. Knowing and so confident, so self-assured, she examined me with her smile. "But there's no place."

"Stay in your room this afternoon." I made plans on the spot. "Say you're sick and I'll do the same."

She looked up at me.

"Blame it on the sea slugs for dinner, or too much Maotai."

Again, her smile. "That wouldn't be fair."

As luck would have it—come to think of things, Tristan and Isolde had crummy luck, too—that afternoon we ended up rehearsing the evening's chestnut in an auditorium filled with dead spots, where sound fails to circulate. But I did manage to sit beside Mira at dinner. Over soup, a viscous affair of sweet globs and bits of mandarin orange, we looked at each other carefully, trying to conceal what we felt.

"The pieces of fat in this rare delicacy are taken from behind the eyes of hibernating frogs, and have great properties for alleviating arthritis in old people," one of the translators explained, relaying our host's words. Half of the time you didn't know whether to laugh or cry. But Mira ate heartily.

At the first opportunity I reached for her knee under the table, and she set her hand on mine for a second. "Not in China," she whispered. "We have to wait until we're home."

Of course I kept repeating "Not in China" until it sounded like some crazy maxim, a Czech's "Never on

Sunday." There had to be a reason for Mira's caution, and the more I pondered it, the more I understood her discreet graciousness. After all, we weren't businessmen at a convention. Since Mira knew all the dressing-room gossip, heard all that could be heard, she obviously saw we had to protect ourselves.

I watched her, counting the days left on tour. Often she looked at someone with the same expression I loved, perhaps a clerk holding out a package or a nervous young waiter, and I ached for her to be looking at me instead. But I took a clue from Mira and made certain no one saw me mooning over her.

And then, almost miraculously, we were home, in a familiar airport, surrounded by flashing bulbs, reporters with questions, television cameras. Families and husbands and wives stood grinning welcome. Why did Pat always look like she'd just come from cleaning the garage? Of course Josef pushed through the crowd, his heavily accented bass calling Mira's name. He took her head in both hands, that wonderful haze of fair hair, enveloping it, crushing it, until I wanted to shout "Stop, you fool, leave her alone." Yet Mira was laughing.

Six incredibly long days passed before the orchestra's next rehearsal. Mira, oh Mira. I telephoned once, Josef answered, I hung up; time dragged; I fantasized, holding the Great Wall photograph close to my face.

Finally that rehearsal came, and after three endless hours I went over to Mira. Eyes glowing, she confided, "My girlfriend's in Florida this month and I'm looking after her plants."

Within the hour we had undressed each other, caressed, touched everywhere, giving ourselves up to love.

For an entire month we used the apartment, filling

its refrigerator with fine Vouvray, and eating ripe brie, grapes, all the pastoral foods. Mira bought new sheets so that we could enjoy ourselves without a care. Nothing would be allowed to stain those afternoons. Recalling them often, I felt renewed and alive. Yet April came, bringing the end of the symphony season and our use of the apartment. I remembered Depression photographs of families standing outside lost homes with their possessions piled high. Mira and I owned only some patterned sheets, which we carried in a paper bag that she patted affectionately while suggesting the gigs. The potential for deception was endless, though we didn't put it quite that way. Only one serious problem remained: we had no place to spread out our sheets.

For our first "rehearsal" we drove to a large park near the edge of the city and made love in my Volvo's back seat. This had a certain high-school inventiveness to it, and Mira liked feeling "so North American," for backseat necking wasn't part of the ordinary Czech adolescence. I, however, twisted my shoulder, and we ended up with Mira massaging the tight muscle. Those long afternoons spent naked took on the quality of a golden age.

As Mira stroked away, I wondered if she'd consider roadside motels part of the North American experience. "Don't you have any more friends on vacation?"

"Remember the Forbidden Palace?"

I nodded.

"I wish we were there now."

"But it was too vast to be romantic. Anyway, they herded us through like . . ."

"It was the first place I thought of you as my lover." She started massaging my shoulder again. "I felt like a Manchu princess, imagining you coming to my room at night."

"You'd have had bound feet."

She massaged harder, remarking thoughtfully, "I wouldn't like that."

The next time we tried a motel, drinking wine out of plastic glasses in order to discard the evidence. But the worn bedspread, ashtray full of someone else's butts and general shabbiness got to us. "Look at it this way," I said consolingly, "the room's nicer than most hotels in China."

Mira snuggled close.

"Imagine we're . . ."

She put her fingers to my lips, stopping me.

At our following meeting, after a genuine re-hearsal, an hour's love talk was all we could manage. Should I have read the future in some gesture? Perhaps when Mira asked, "Did you call me at home yesterday? And hang up when Josef answered?"

I hadn't. "No. It must have been a wrong number."

"We have to be careful."

"But I never called you, Mira."

I couldn't telephone her at home, and she couldn't call me either. Sometimes I stared at my phone, enraged that it mocked me by sitting there. If I couldn't reach Mira, why have a phone at all? And yet I caught myself waiting for it to ring, hoping her voice would answer mine.

Suddenly Pat began cooking a rash of chop suey dinners. "Why do we have to eat this?" I complained.

"You keep talking about China so I bought a wok."

Just what I needed, a wife anxious to please. I felt almost ashamed.

After the next rehearsal Mira and I drove to a Chinese area of town and ambled along the streets. There were only a few other non-Orientals around, university types into cheap ethnic food or perhaps lovers trying to hide out. We picked a small restaurant with formica tabletops and embroidered Chinese landscapes on the walls. Fingering her chopsticks, Mira looked about with pleasure. "I hope this place never gets discovered. The whites will ruin it."

"I want to be in bed with you," I said, ignoring the menu.

"And I'd like some hot-and-sour soup." She tapped my knuckles with the chopstick. "Tim, we can't do anything about that today. Let's not spoil the time we have."

Properly chastised, I saw myself as overbearing and difficult. "I'm sorry."

"While we're here let's go into one of the shops for some hoisin sauce. I'm learning to cook Chinese—it's really a healthy way to eat. Yesterday I bought a wok."

I took a swig of hot tea and burned my mouth.

Mira went on to say that she and Josef planned to fly down to New York for a long weekend. The Plaza was having a special and they enjoyed its old world elegance.

"Have I done something wrong, Mira?"

She shook her head while I fought off a series of images: Josef and Mira on their way home from the theatre; Josef and Mira drinking brandy nightcaps in the Palm Court; Josef unbuttoning Mira's silk blouse, unclasping her coral necklace, slipping off . . .

"Of course not, Tim."

I could hear that hokey Palm Court violinist playing the theme song from *Gigi*.

I went home with a terrible headache and stood under a hot shower, letting the water shoot into my back, into my neck, while turning my head slowly to ease the muscles. I looked down at my body: Mira should have

81

been touching it.

Delayed at work, Pat phoned to say I'd find leftover fried rice in the refrigerator. I poured myself a double scotch, drank it neat and stared at the telephone. Picking up the receiver, I dialled Mira's number but hung up before her phone had the chance to ring. I thought of asking Pat for a divorce and I thought of ordering in pizza and then I thought the best thing would be to practise my oboe. What amazed me was that Mira could want what she had. So what if you're in love with one man and your husband suggests a weekend at the Plaza? Enjoy the Plaza. Simple peasant logic, not the least bit complicated. Mira knew her power as a woman, which meant the day would provide.

Upstairs, in my studio, I sat for half an hour with oboe in hand, a score spread out reproachfully on the music stand. I was vaguely studying my bare feet when the idea hit. If I quickly pulled on a sweatshirt and some Adidas, I could drive over to Mira's and watch her leave. If, in fact, she was going anywhere.

In twenty minutes I parked outside Mira's, glaring at the flashy apartment building Josef had chosen—a perfect setting for one of his diatribes. What if Mira looked out and spotted my Volvo? I slid down in my seat. Suddenly the lights in Mira's went off. Hardly breathing, I slipped down farther, and just in time, for the doorman came out carrying luggage, followed by Josef, and then Mira. I couldn't see if she smiled. In an instant they climbed into a waiting taxi.

If Mira could do this, I didn't know the least bit about her. Worse, even, I didn't know that I understood anything better for spying, though I kept thinking about what I might have learned until Tuesday's rehearsal. Mira wore a new floppy straw hat, the sort women always have in impressionist paintings of picnic lunches, and I realized that everyone liked to have Mira with them, so her husband would hardly be the exception—he'd married her, after all. Suddenly I felt an odd comradeship with Josef, as if we weren't rivals but men with a common passion. Which immediately made me wonder about other comrades in arms, as yet unknown.

A stroke of fortune left Mira in charge of another friend's apartment, and she told me with a gleam in her eyes. We hurried there after the rehearsal. Mira's touch, smiles, attention, Mira's power over me, banished all recriminations. Once again I became her devoted lover.

"I missed you," she whispered into my chest hair.

"I'll believe it if you want me to."

"Oh, Timothy, why do you like to hurt me?"

No one, not even my parents, called me Timothy.

"I'm sorry, Mira, I never mean it like that. You've got to see how . . ." I resolved not to accuse her any more, not to complain or expect attention. I couldn't understand, but I could love.

The success of my new approach cheered me, and naturally relieved Mira, who responded with an ardour that equalled mine. I felt confident of our future, without imagining what it would be like. After a rehearsal with Old Musick, Mira waited for me in the parking lot. She wore a white sundress with small black polka dots, and red sandals; she glistened.

"The more I study it, the more bloated this score seems." I waved the Schubert mass we'd just played.

"You've got to stop phoning me at home."

"What are you talking about?"

"The caller who hangs up."

"Maybe you've caught the fancy of someone in the audience. Like that crazy who kept sending roses to

Adele before each concert."

"No one's sending flowers. Just hanging up."

"But why assume it's me?"

She frowned rather harshly, I felt, considering my innocence.

"Josef suspects. I'm sure he does, and I can't have that."

"Did he say anything about . . ."

"No," she cut me off. "You've gotten too attached, Timothy. Don't you understand? You're spoiling what might . . ."

"Spoiling? Damn it, Mira, I'm in love with you."

She surveyed the parking lot. "Let's sit in my car."

Hot air poured out when we opened the doors.

"We can't see each other any more," Mira began calmly. "I decided last night."

"What?"

"We can be friends, Tim. But you're too attached."

"If you'll leave Josef I'll leave Pat," I blurted out.

"I couldn't hurt Josef."

"This is crazy."

"See? That's just what I mean—you don't understand." Mira sighed.

"What is it you want me to understand?"

"If you don't already, there's nothing I can explain." She ran one hand through her hair, shaking her head. "I thought you were different from this. It's all my fault."

"Mira, please."

"Let's just go back to the way we were before China."

"Mira, listen to me."

"You'd better go." She looked out at the parking

lot again. "We've got to be careful." Then she turned toward me and set her hand on my arm, like a nurse in a ward for terminal patients. "Don't look at me like that, Tim. I'm sorry it has to be this way. For a while we . . ." She stopped, possibly overwhelmed by the sadness of life.

I wondered if she believed I'd made the calls; if, in fact, there were any calls; if Josef suspected. If, if, if . . . I got out and closed the door slowly, stammering "Mira," but she flipped on the ignition.

I spent the rest of the day wandering about the city, dreading the sight of my home, a little museum of married shopping, with its Sunday-auction antiques. And nothing to blame this on but my own weakness. Shape up, I kept telling myself. You're unhinged. See Mira tonight; talk with her; convince her. She wants you to convince her, of course. A woman like Mira deserves as much.

That evening the orchestra gathered in a small room off the chancel and began to enter the church, a few at a time and in no particular order. Tuning-up noises filled the air as I took my place. Almost immediately Mira came in with another cellist. Though all the women dressed alike, Mira looked more dramatic than the rest. She wore her long black skirt and white silk blouse with flair, not as work clothes. I felt my throat tighten. Her hair seemed gold in the church's muted light.

The audience chattered in uncomfortable pews, rustling their programs as the choir filed into the chancel steps. My mouth burned. Mira never even glanced my way. Surrounded by people, I stared as she sat absorbed in her cello. Then, silence. The conductor stepped out, followed by four soloists, who took their places. We began Schubert's ominous chords, repeating them until a melody emerged. It hung in the vast space.

I couldn't take another moment. Holding my oboe

to my chest, I shouted "No." This filled the air terribly, and was so unexpected that everyone seemed to miss it. The orchestra kept playing and the choir continued in Latin. But my "No" echoed, coming back on itself, reverberating over and over. Firm and decisive and bleak. "No."

I stumbled out of the wind section while maybe half the orchestra kept playing. People stood up, I think. But I didn't care. I ran through the chancel into the men's room and went into one of the stalls, still clutching my oboe as I leaned against its partition.

Someone opened the men's room door. "Are you okay?" A familiar voice. Barry's.

"Yes."

"Are you sick?"

"Go away."

"Tim, what's wrong?"

"Go away, Barry."

The door opened again. I didn't know how many people were gathering outside my stall.

"Go away."

"Tim?" Pat's voice. "Are you all right?"

I reached inside my coat pocket for the photograph Barry had taken on the Great Wall. Mira and I, barely touching, stared into the camera. She half smiled, her wonderful smile of concealment.

"Tim?"

"Go away."

Mira and I, side by side, against those ancient Chinese mountains. I took the photograph and tore it in half, then in half again, and once more, in shreds, and then I dropped the pieces into the toilet bowl, and flushed. "Goddamn you, Mira."

"What?" Pat cried, pounding the door. Then she gasped. "I knew it. I knew there was someone."

More people hurried into the men's room and as its door opened again I could hear the orchestra begin Schubert's Kyrie.

"Please, Tim," Barry said.

"He's harmless," a voice called from somewhere above me, and I looked up to see a pair of eyes at the top of the partition scanning for razor blades, or perhaps an empty pill bottle. Harmless, I thought.

"Tim?" Pat sobbed.

"Stop it. I can't even go to the john without you around."

Somebody pounded the stall's door again; voices whispered. Out in the chancel Mira would be waiting for her solo, shoulders back, eyes partly closed, expression intent.

"Everything will be okay," Barry tried to calm me.

Sure it would. I had nothing to fear from Mira, not even love.

Tale of Woe

Juan Acuna had only meant to be clever when he named the bird Tale of Woe, but now, Tale of Woe was dead. Black-feathered, with purple and green and yellow markings, it lay on one side in the bottom of a two-foot-high antique wicker birdcage shaped like a pagoda. Iva Vranic had suggested the birdcage. Dr. Iva Vranic. (*"Eva Vra-ish,* Juan. Forget the spelling.") The birdcage had to be an expensive one, a genuine commitment, in order to work. In spite of doubts, he went along with her. And now look. Poor Tale of Woe had plucked out some fine black feathers from its breast and, in a moment of despair, plunged its sharp beak into the flesh, committing suicide like anyone else with a broken heart.

La mierda, Juan muttered, backing away from the cage. *Estoy jodido.* He reached into his shirt for the small amulet hanging from a chain around his neck, clasped it as Mamacita would have held her crucifix and then opened it, letting a fine, dry, brownish powder fall into his hand. He touched the powder.

Maybe, Juan thought, he should have gone for broke and bought the toucan. But sixteen hundred bucks. Yet how could a myna ever be the right substitute! Maybe he'd unconsciously wished to kill Tale of Woe, or Mamacita, or himself.

Or Beige, damn Beige.

Juan sighed, touching the powder absent-mindedly. Beige loved the stuff—they all did—and he was running low. They loved playing with the amulet, fingering it in his black chest hair, and he loved watching their surprised expressions when he explained, "It's my home. Earth from Argentina. From Cordoba, where I grew up. Cordoba. The oldest colonial city in Argentina." Once a week or so Juan had to refill the amulet from a mason jar of dirt he kept in a bureau drawer. He never showed the jar, though he'd been tempted to. Especially with his recent Beige. (Juan called all fairish Canadian women "Beige," which he pronounced "*Bahy*-jzhe," making two syllables of it; they loved this, too.)

Mynas were risky. The pet-shop owner had sold him a book about them, and Juan had read it carefully. Great mimics, mynas also formed deep attachments and, if neglected, fell into depression, stopped eating, sometimes stabbed themselves to death. Juan had kept watching for signs, but Tale of Woe's appetite never flagged. And every day he spent at least thirty minutes before work and half an hour after dinner with his hand in the extravagant cage, getting to know Tale of Woe. Building trust and confidence. He'd even taught it *"Gracias, muchacho."*

Juan frowned, sniffing the dry earth. If he hadn't gone off for the long Easter weekend with Beige, Tale of Woe might still be jumping from one perch to another. . . . He stepped toward the cage and reached inside. Never before had Juan realized how much life the elegant plumage contained. Now the bird offered no resistance to his hand, no pecks or nervous cries.

For a moment Juan stared at his marvellous friend, then went into the kitchen, where he wrapped it first in an old dishtowel, and after in Alcoa foil. Unsure of his next move, he set Tale of Woe on the bottom shelf of the refrigerator.

"How does that make you feel, Juan?"

As Dr. Vranic put the question during their regular Monday session, Juan struggled with himself. "It's my luck. A weekend in the country leaves me with another failure."

Iva Vranic nodded.

"Maybe I'll never learn to be responsible."

"And how does that make you feel?"

"Estoy jodido."

"What?"

"I'm fucked."

She nodded again. "Would you like to work on this?"

Juan eyed the old tennis racket on a carpet-covered box beside him, which he sometimes used during gestalts to beat out old anger.

"I can't adjust, and I'll never be responsible until I adjust." He shuddered as he said the word. "Anyway, how can an exile adjust? I think of home, and Videla's coup, and wonder if I'll ever go back. What have I got here? I studied design at the best theatre school in Argentina, and nobody cares. Laying out advertising copy— some life for a revolutionary! With one woman after another playing that dumb song from *Evita* to remind me of home. *Es la mierda.*

"It's shit. And don't ask me how I feel about that. A revolutionary belongs with his people. Believe me, nothing important has happened since '76. I designed a poster for theatre in the factories and Videla took over before it even got printed. But you can't understand." He sighed. "I would go back and fight, but party discipline runs my life." He glared at Iva Vranic. "And one should

91

resist emotionalism."

"For three months, Juan, you've been attacking emotionalism. Do you think you might have an investment in making therapy fail?"

"Revolutionaries don't need therapy."

"Then why are you here?"

Just like Mamacita, boxing him into a corner. Juan recalled his parents' beautiful bourgeois house in Cordoba, with closed-off rooms seldom entered in order to preserve their decorum. "Juanito went in," his brother Raoul would accuse at dinner.

"You're stupid, Iva. Why are you so stupid?" He loved asking this because she never reacted.

Lips tight, Dr. Vranic sat crosslegged in yoga fashion. Long brown hair, now greying, fell over her shoulders in a style unchanged since her college days thirty years ago. Such plainness made Juan sad. Why, he wondered, did she just stare? Of course he was unusually handsome—every Beige said as much. Dark, charming, romantic. And he always smelled of Spanish lavender water. Perhaps Iva admired his new leather sportcoat?

"No one's ever called you a spic, Iva."

She shook her head. "Who called you that, Juan?"

"They think it."

"I see." She paused. "Juan, I grew up in Yugoslavia, during the war, and when I left Ljubljana to come here and live with an aunt, I felt lonely too."

"You were from Europe, Iva. Canadians feel fine about that. Europe's okay."

She nodded. "We're nearly out of time and I wonder why you avoid talking about Tale of Woe? How do you feel about that?"

"I like your voice, Iva. It doesn't hurt my ears. These Canadian girls are high and squeaky, so loud, high and squeaky. Or else mumbling."

"Yes?"

He sat back, flecking bits of cracked leather from the arm of an old easy chair. "Did anyone ever say that you coo? Almost like your voice comes up underneath a word to embrace it."

Iva Vranic started looking away.

"*Hola*. Listen to me. I can do two things—remember and wait. When Raoul was shot after the coup, neighbour ladies brought us food, cakes, fruit, while my family mourned. The ladies couldn't help Raoul, but at least they did something. All the men could do was remember and wait."

"Tale of Woe brings up your brother?"

"Maybe I should have ordered that toucan from New York. They eat fruit, you know." He briefly fingered his gold amulet. "But the myna was a beginning."

Iva Vranic smiled. "We must find a way for you to grieve," she commented, her tone matter-of-fact yet warm. "And release anger. . . ."

Juan tuned out, listening to the sound of Iva Vranic's voice.

How do you mourn a pet myna? After leaving Dr. Vranic, Juan brooded on this question all night. By the next session, he had a curiously triumphant feeling about his answer.

"I've got a plan, Iva. I'm going to make . . ."

"Take a deep breath, Juan," she cautioned. "And feel where you are."

"I'm going to make a fantastic big bird," he started up again, impatient. "A costume."

Iva Vranic looked attentively at Juan.

"I'll design it out of papier-mâché and black velvet, and maybe feathers, too. A bird like Tale of Woe, beautiful and sleek."

"Yes?" Iva Vranic took several long drags on her cigarette.

"You have to help it come to life, Iva. It needs a heart. So you'll wear the costume when we bury Tale of Woe."

"And how will this help, Juan?"

"I owe it a decent burial."

Iva Vranic nodded.

"Near my apartment. In Queen's Park."

"All I have to do is wear the costume?"

"That's right. You're the heart. The life. But no one will see that, except me. They'll see Tale of Woe come back like the Phoenix."

"As long as we can do it during your therapy hour. . . ."

Juan immediately began planning the costume. He borrowed library books with bright illustrations of birds so that his sketches would be perfect, and after a late evening at his drafting board, had one that satisfied him. If not an exact likeness of Tale of Woe, it would do: the costume consisted of a papier-mâché head, its feathered part covered with black velvet, the heavy curling beak painted deep yellow. Shiny glass eyes were essential. But how would Iva see? After puzzling about this, Juan decided to find a gold chain and drape it about the bird's neck, a chain long enough so that he could hold onto one end, like a leash. The costume's head would fit over Iva's and be sewn to a loose black robe with wings for sleeves.

In a burst of good humour, Juan shopped for wire, paste, cloth, thread and plain white feathers, which he dyed the exact shades of purple and yellow and green. He assembled the costume while singing aloud, each detail carefully planned, each stitch expertly tailored. The emerging costume had a carnival gaiety, but Juan still wasn't satisfied and worked harder, adding more detail, putting a third coat of shellac on the beak until it glistened. The gold chain added one last loving touch.

Iva Vranic gasped when Juan showed her the costume. "I had no idea," she stammered. "It's beautiful."

Beaming, Juan outlined their itinerary: Saturday morning, at ten o'clock, Iva would arrive at his apartment in the Manulife Centre, and they would begin the slow walk to Queen's Park. "Then I'll accept my guilt," he explained.

"Isn't it enough to make the costume?"

Juan shook his head, amazed at her stupidity. "Iva, Iva, you don't understand."

On Saturday, a taxi pulled up before Juan's building. Already waiting in the lobby, he came out with the bird costume over his arm and Tale of Woe in a Florsheim shoebox. "Are you embarrassed, Iva?"

"Of course. But let me have it. I'm due at my office by noon."

She pulled the costume over her head as Juan held the bird's beak in one hand, the back of its skull with the other. Yards of black velvet fell to cover Iva Vranic's sweater and jeans, and all that remained of her were orthopedic sandals poking out at the bottom of the robe.

"I can't see, Juan." Layers of papier-mâché and cloth muffled her voice.

Juan stood back, astonished to see the bird come to life. His throat tightened. "I'm ready," he said, tugging the golden leash.

As Juan walked toward Bloor, he felt the muscles in his neck and back open up, his body stretching taller. A car honked, and he waved. "We're at a curb," he said toward the beak. The gigantic bird stopped still, and when

Juan pulled the leash, it timidly moved across the street. Juan felt proud of himself for doing things right. After the funeral, he'd spend the money, take a risk. He'd order the toucan from New York. An extravagant bird, Juan smiled to think. He would call it Heart's Ease.

Another horn blew and the myna's head bobbed up and down.

The warm April morning had brought out shoppers, lovers and street crazies. Juan felt everyone's eyes turned in his direction.

"What're ya selling?" called a young man.

Juan lifted his chin.

Several teenagers passed, and one snickered. "Craz-ee. That one should see my shrink."

Juan continued forward, holding the leash tightly.

"Mommie, look. Mommie, look. It's Big Bird." A small girl shouted gleefully and reached out toward the velvet robe.

"Go away," Juan croaked.

"Is Ernie here too?" the girl asked.

As Juan continued past the Colonnade, more stares and laughter surrounded him. "Leave us alone," he growled at a group of boys clustered near the myna. But people turned to watch, waiting for the bird to reveal its purpose.

"Caw caw caw," one of the boys cried, flapping his arms.

"Caw caw," another picked up the chant.

The myna's head bobbed from side to side.

"Go away," Juan groaned. There must have been several dozen people gathering.

Fifty feet ahead, near the large intersection, a policeman stood with a bag lady in satin.

"Caw caw caw."

Juan dropped his leash just as the policeman

noticed this growing crow. *Estoy jodido*, he whispered, drawing quickly away from Iva Vranic.

"What's going on here?" the policeman called.

Iva Vranic flailed about in her velvet robes, pushing the myna head up and off. But her arms, caught in the sleeves, couldn't untangle themselves at first, and then with one quick thrust everybody saw jeans emerge from ankle to knee to waist, until a plump middle-aged woman stood before them holding onto the hem of a vast black robe. The myna's head lay at her feet, on the sidewalk.

"What is it, lady?" Bewildered, the policeman reached for her arm.

"Let me go," Iva Vranic snapped. "I've got to find my patient."

"Your what?"

"My patient, don't you see?" Flushed from the airless costume, she began to wheeze as she gulped several deep breaths.

"It's all right, lady, I'll help you."

"He can't be far."

"Your patient? Could I see some ID, please?"

Iva Vranic stared into his bland pink smile. "I'm a therapist." She began looking about for Juan.

"Uh-huh. How would you like to sit in my patrol car for a little rest?"

"Perdón, Perdón," Juan begged into the telephone receiver when Iva Vranic called his apartment later that day. "I see a uniform and have to run."

"We'll talk about it during your Monday appointment," she answered, less consoling than usual.

After hanging up, Juan imagined Iva Vranic led off by police, stripped of the bird costume, tied to a nasty chair and beaten with the butt of a gun until she gave his name. But of course she wouldn't. Poor Iva, roughed up in one of the secret police cells that every *Star* reporter would give a year's salary to photograph, all for befriending a revolutionary like himself. He thought of those gentle, strong-willed nuns who kept hand grenades under their habits because they knew the difference between right and wrong. Iva was like that, suffering humiliation on his account. Iva, Iva. He imagined her before him, listening intently while smoking her cigarette. He wondered, for the first time, what her breasts looked like. Poor, gentle Iva.

Iva Vranic's home answering machine promised a return call, but Juan hung up when it started beeping: no sensible man left his voice on a recording device.

Without considering why, Juan drove toward Iva Vranic's apartment. He'd often wondered what sort of place she lived in, and now found an old pseudo-Tudor building, much less prepossessing than he had imagined. Its hallway smelled of fresh paint and cooked cabbage (the cabbage, at least, seemed right), and at her door Juan slowly read the hand-lettered card—Dr. Iva Vranic—in neat European script. Poor, sweet Iva. He knocked. Did a bird chirp inside? No answer. His jacket pockets were empty—neither pen nor paper—but as Juan searched in his shirt pocket he felt a lump: the gold amulet. He slipped its chain over his head, refusing to look at his trembling hands, and quickly knelt down to push the gift under Iva Vranic's door. It fit, barely.

I've done the right thing, Juan consoled himself, hurrying home to await her call.

The afternoon passed and by seven o'clock Juan realized that Iva Vranic might not have recognized his gift, even if she'd already found it. He telephoned, blurting out, "Did you get my present? Are you all right?"

"Ah, Juan!" Iva Vranic seemed relieved. "It's a lovely charm, but I can't accept . . ."

"I want you to."

"We'll talk about this on Monday."

"Don't hang up, Iva."

"Juan, is anything wrong?"

"I just want to see you. Psychiatrists in movies always come out in the middle of the night."

Iva Vranic laughed.

"You see," Juan coaxed, "I made you feel better."

"Well yes," she admitted. "That charm was puzzling, though."

"Charm? Iva, Iva, sometimes you amaze me." Juan explained how to unscrew the amulet, which she promised to try after they hung up.

Putting down the receiver, Juan felt lonely and beaten. He could easily call Beige, or find a new one. Damn Beige. In his bureau drawer he found the mason jar of dirt and poured a mound in the palm of his hand. Tonight it didn't work; he couldn't believe. The dirt, in fact, came from cottage country north of the city. Juan remembered the day he'd filled the jar, after reading a paperback thriller whose exotic heroine kept a clump of Mother Russia in her jewel box. Well, the Beiges liked it—good for something. He sighed.

Yet lying to Iva Vranic was like lying to himself, so Juan prepared the sacrifice. He wrote a card—

Dear Iva.
This fantasy of mine must come to an end. The earth I'm giving you is from a friend's vegetable garden in Muskoka, not from Argentina. But you will understand why I needed to believe in it, and why I want you to have it now.   Juan

99

—and attached it to the jar with a bit of red ribbon. Then he drove back to Iva Vranic's and, without knocking, left this outside her door.

At their Monday afternoon session, Iva Vranic handed over the gold amulet. "You mustn't leave any more presents for me."

Resigned, Juan slipped it around his neck.

"How do you feel about my returning this?"

"Did you bring the earth, too?"

She shook her head.

"Then you understood, Iva. I could love a woman like you."

That night Juan ordered a dozen long-stemmed roses to be delivered to Iva Vranic's apartment.

"You have to stop, Juan."

"Don't you like roses?"

"You're missing the point."

Then he sent an orchid plant.

"Please, stop," Iva Vranic pleaded during their next hour.

His shoulders slumped in disappointment.

After the session, Juan filled a mason jar with dirt from Queen's Park, wrote a card saying, "You only like earth," and left this outside Iva Vranic's apartment.

"Juan, when you were a boy, did you put surprise gifts around the house for your mother?"

"Of course not. We hardly ever had surprises at home."

"And how did you feel about that, Juan?"

"Don't you see, Iva, I'm falling in love with you."

She leaned back, crossing her arms.

"Well, it doesn't matter?"

"How do you feel about my silence?" she replied.

"I know what you're thinking, that I ran away and

deserted you. But I saw that policeman coming and the gun he was wearing."

"He didn't have a gun, Juan."

"Are you sure? It makes me think of Raoul. Raoul's nice clean bullet. Did I ever tell you that when the undertakers laid out his body, they found Raoul's balls had been cut off?" He watched Iva Vranic's eyes grow wide. "What Canadian believes in anything so much he'd lose his balls?"

"I can't answer for them, but my father fought in the Yugoslav resistance along with . . ."

"You're a beautiful woman, Iva. Did anyone tell you that lately? Sometimes you're as beautiful as my mother. She had sad eyes too."

"Our time's almost up for today, Juan."

Troubled, Juan spent the weekend missing Iva Vranic. He thought of increasing his therapy from three to four hours a week. Iva seemed to like him so she'd probably find time. But by Sunday night Juan knew what he really wanted.

After showering, shaving and carefully picking out his clothes, Juan headed for Iva Vranic's apartment, a bottle of Chilean wine tucked under his arm.

"Ah!" she exclaimed at her door. "Has something happened?"

"May I come in?"

She wore a corduroy housecoat and had her hair pinned up in a heavy knob. Juan saw that her feet were bare.

"Yes, yes, Of course."

He had never imagined such an apartment. His Iva had lived with plants and sunshine and air, maybe a strain of Chopin or some classical guitar, but not these heavy dark antiques—there must have been five occasional tables covered in clutter—and dark wooden icons glaring from the walls.

"Would you like to sit?"

"*Sí.*" He passed her the wine.

Trying to remember their evening the next day, Juan felt confused. He couldn't recall much of the conversation, or how one thing led to another, but saw a bottle of brandy, a half-empty glass and several books open on the sofa. As Iva Vranic bent to move them, Juan reached out for her shoulders and drew her around, then close. Shocked, they held still. Were they alone in the world? "Iva, Iva," he whispered, slipping his hand inside her housecoat. More nipple than flesh, he thought. "Do you know what we're doing?"

Iva Vranic kept her face buried against his chest.

"Iva?"

"We'll talk about it later."

"In my session?" he teased.

"I'm divorced, Juan. You've heard about divorcées."

Her housecoat was open now, and Juan knelt down, running his hand over her stomach. "I didn't know you were married."

"Until last year." She hesitated. "But I don't want to talk about it."

He kept stroking. "Oh Beige, Beige, you're a beauty, a sphinx."

Pulling her down to the sofa, for the first time Juan noticed his myna costume neatly laid out, its head propped so that the beak curled over the seat of an antique chair.

"You have to keep our bird," Juan whispered, using the toe of one shoe to kick off the other. "And take good care of it."

They made love that night, and the next one too, but not during Juan's therapy sessions, where he and Iva

Vranic scrupulously kept to the agenda. "Why is it you know so much about me?" Juan asked, sadly, at the end of their Monday hour. And later that night, while helping Iva Vranic out of her blouse, "Let's see each other, okay, but let's make sure we don't fall in love?" She didn't reply.

"It's hard to have a high opinion of the human race," Juan offered during Wednesday's hour. "Mostly I'd rather have a pack of wolves around any day. *Entiendes?* If we're the highest creation, God was no genius."

"You can't mean that?" Iva Vranic asked, jotting something on the pad she kept beside her.

Bristling, Juan attempted a good-natured smile. He expected women to believe what they were told. "I don't think we're becoming lovers."

"And how do you feel about that, Juan?"

His black eyes flashed like sparklers at Mardi Gras. "Do I have to feel about it?" Once the words came out, Juan glared at this small compact woman, almost squat, really, who looked like one of the maids from his childhood.

"Juan?"

"I came to you so that I could find out what love is like. It was my reason for starting therapy."

"And?"

He looked out the window, from which he could see the back of a Portuguese store beside the old house where Iva Vranic had her office. Sun glistened on the yard filled with wooden crates and at least six garbage cans. Then a door opened and someone walked out. Tall, ample, with olive skin, a woman of about forty stood on the top step, letting sun pour onto her uplifted face and throat. She wiped her forehead with the back of one hand, a gesture that made Juan ache, and stretched like a cat called from napping. The woman kept stretching, yawning, and now rubbed her bare arms, as if she could work the sun into a lather. Black blouse and skirt, stained apron, red slippers, all were transformed by her yearning, her need.

"Juan?"

He turned.

"Our hour's almost over."

Of course, of course! All Iva wanted was his money.

"I'll come by tonight," he said.

Juan arrived in a dark mood, and settled on the sofa without a moment's small talk. "It's not easy for me, Iva, but I have to say something." She joined him, and Juan noticed fine earrings and make-up she never wore during therapy sessions. "I don't think we should sleep together again . . ." He stopped because of something in her eyes. "What is it, Iva? What are you feeling?"

She leaned back into a cushion.

"Iva, why did you sleep with me?"

"We had to get through that, Juan, so you could go on with your therapy."

His hands trembled. "That's all? I thought you liked it."

She reached toward his arm. "I have a present for you, Juan."

He froze as Iva Vranic took a small crystal jar from the cluttered coffee table. "It's Yugoslavian."

"What?"

"The earth inside. From Ljubljana. I've kept it for twenty-five years, since I left home." She held the jar toward him.

"I'm getting out of here."

He rose and dashed across the room in a single motion.

Flatly, she called, "Your appointment's tomorrow

104

at five."

"Puta, puta," he cried, his face red.

After slamming the door, Juan stood staring at its perfectly lettered card. *Whore!* He waited, but the door didn't open. A cold, heartless one, mocking him like that. Probably still laughing! He had to see for sure.

Juan left the hall and made his way around her building, night and the shrubbery hiding him. His heart pounded as he reached the windows of Iva Vranic's apartment, and peered in.

Iva Vranic stood in front of the vanity, leaning toward its mirror with lips parted, like a woman being wooed. She stayed this way until Juan felt the muscles in his legs strain from pulling up toward the window ledge. Suddenly Iva turned from the mirror and reached into her closet. Out came the myna costume. She slipped its velvet robe over her head, disappearing under a black billow. Next, she lifted the head over her own and settled in slowly. A perfect fit. The black hulk began to sway, rocking back and forth, the myna's head bobbing. Did she hear a sob through the open window?

Back and forth bobbed the head, back and forth.

Rain for the Weekend

They arrived soaking wet from the parking lot. She didn't say "You promised sun."

"Think of this as *Rebecca* weather," he apologized, shrugging with a slight impish smile.

She laughed in spite of herself, and the wet curls plastered to her head. "Some start for a weekend in the country."

In their case the country meant a fashionable inn an hour's drive from the city—once an old stone gristmill, now an elegant restaurant and guestrooms full of antiques. "Landscaped grounds, outdoor pool and exercise facilities add diversion to romance," claimed the brochure Matt had given Susan. Here women moved smoothly, dressing with flair, as if each considered herself Irene Dunne holing up with Cary Grant in a smart old comedy. Of course the Mill had a cellar of consequence.

"We owe it to ourselves," Matt Dwyer had told Susan Hilliard, suggesting this trip. She had agreed eagerly.

They'd met at a conference two months before. When Matt asked if she was reading a paper, Susan answered, "I specialize in splendid accommodations, the best catered meals, simultaneous translations, easy-going tour-guides and telephone numbers for all catastrophes."

107

They spent the night together. Her warmth in bed showed Matt how Susan could organize conferences for such varied groups as medical researchers, oil industrialists, Amnesty lawyers or, in his case, psychiatrists: she valued the nuances of a man's pleasure.

They both knew that the first weekend away together was a trial run, though of course you didn't mention this. The stages of unpacking offered a way to steady themselves. Susan approved of their room, surveying its subdued blend of Persian rugs, sleek modern furniture and *objets*. Taste, she reflected, is an accomplishment. While setting out her perfume and make-up on the bathroom vanity, noting well-designed rose-coloured plumbing, she could see Matt reflected in the mirror-covered wall as he hung slacks in a closet. It made her smile to watch him smooth out one resistant crease, a frown on his open face. She began to hum *I get a kick out of you.*

"We could take a walk, there's only light drizzle," Matt suggested.

Susan went on humming, but louder.

"Or that," he laughed.

Then she laughed too. "The bed's not going anywhere."

"Better not," he replied, now leaning against the bathroom door-frame to watch her. This was the first time he'd seen Susan adjusting her make-up, and something made him draw away. It was as if she were joining the long line of women observed, back from Ruth, his ex-wife, to college romances, high-school crushes and his mother, in lacy white silk slip, powdering her face before going out for the evening: powder, perfume, the rustle of skirts and clasping of jewellery always meant women were about to leave you. "I'd like to walk," he said after a moment.

"There are umbrellas in the lobby. And the rain's warm."

But they ended up at a window table in the lounge, blue-grey light filtering intimacy around them. They stared at each other, as if to discover why this particular confluence of atoms had inspired such infatuation. They sipped drinks, then sipped again. Matt dragged at his cigarette. The woman before him had dried her hair carefully, yet a few curls resisted, holding just enough dampness to make him want to take them between his fingers, his lips. Her mouth, a trifle too wide, had been tamed with pale lip gloss of the same pinkish colour she'd expertly brushed on her eyelids. Afternoon colours, he guessed, remembering that her eyelids became the palest silvery grey in the evening. She had the right features for high romance.

But for no apparent reason, Matt found himself thinking: You don't change the heart with new clothing.

"Do you want to walk?" Susan asked. No, she thought, he really wants to talk about himself. Fortunately she wanted to listen: this is why they had come away from the city. The first weekend with Seth had rained like this, too. *Happy the bride that the sun shines upon.* Yet Seth and Matt were different—she repeated this thought—and she'd never been a bride. Though two years of living with Seth must have qualified her for some title. My god, she suddenly realized, Matt was talking to her in full earnest.

"Susan, I've published one book and a couple of monographs and lecture monthly at the Institute. But it all feels like writing up lab notes on a dead body. White culture's finished. And more and more I wonder if anyone will bother to study us a few centuries from now, the way we have Sanskrit experts."

She turned away, noticing a handsome fiftyish couple enter the lounge. "You've got to believe in something, no?"

Matt took up the pitcher beside him. "Do you want more sangria?"

She shook her head. Though the room was nearly empty, a maître d' seated the couple two tables away. Well dressed, the man and woman struck Susan as elegant, even admirable. Perhaps he practised law while she worked as a film producer.

"What does that look mean?" Matt asked.

"I'm trying to figure you out," Susan replied, reaching for her glass after all.

With a slightly sardonic smile, Matt said, "I gave up on that long ago. It's one of the profession's fringe benefits." He paused, feeling that her idealism took the edge off simple pleasure. "Have you ever thought of killing yourself?"

Susan shook her head. So he was bringing out the whole arsenal.

Matt looked toward the window.

"Does that mean something's wrong with me?" she replied.

"Well, maybe a certain lack of imagination."

She laughed, embarrassed.

"The other day I was talking with a patient about definitions of mankind," he went on. "You know all the old ones. 'Man's the animal who thinks.' Or reasons, or makes clay pots. Whatever. Well, it hit me that man's the only animal capable of believing it shouldn't exist."

"Don't monkeys commit suicide? I read . . ."

"That's not the point, Susan. What I'm getting at is . . ." He stopped, reaching for a cigarette. "I'm sorry, don't listen to me. Not when I get in one of my apocalyptic moods."

She assumed that the weary smile crossing his

face was an apocalyptic one, and considered the word *apocalyptic*: you read it often enough these days but people seldom spoke it. Maybe born-again preachers or priests did, but who knew any of those? Matt's tone conveyed the melancholy appropriate to his profession. Like other men she'd met at his convention, men with pensive, languid faces, Matt had a vast perspective on the mind's sufferings; Susan actually preferred the hopeful steadiness of church workers raising funds for the Boat People—they might drink perfectly awful things like rum and Coke, but their smiles were less uneasy, less insistent.

The way Matt dragged on his cigarette made her recall Seth once more. After their affair he continued to phone every six months, gradually becoming a permanent casual reality in her life. He'd phoned again this morning while she waited for Matt—"Just to hear your news." Something in Seth's voice, so eager to charm, a child's eagerness, made her yearn for higher innocence, but she knew Seth couldn't draw her back to that time, and a commitment less to him than to her own faithfulness. Oh give it a rest, she thought.

Matt took Susan's hand. She loved him, he knew, without having to think about it. "Let's undress, and cuddle," he said, almost reflectively.

Back in their room, Susan's smooth tanned shoulder brushed against Matt's smooth tanned chest as he stood behind her, arms about her naked waist, while she pulled off the bedspread and top sheet. "Or we could do more than cuddle," he whispered into her hair.

Atoms moved wildly, some named Matt, some Susan, some, more simply, bed. Joy is a strange emotion: atoms in abandon. Susan is Susan, then Matt, then bed; Matt is Susan, Matt, bed; bed is all.

"We're something!" exclaimed Matt.

111

They slept before dinner, a blurred, warm gesture toward monotony and peace. Another welcome stage in steadying themselves. Then, preparations, the sense of occasion mounting as Susan slipped on her dress, awaiting Matt's gasp.

When he stepped out of the bathroom, wearing only briefs, Matt faced a living illustration from an issue of *Vogue* circa 1928. Susan stood at the foot of their unmade bed in an antique tube dress covered with shimmering bugle beads. The waist, dropped low, flattered her slimness, and a gauzy panelled skirt hung longer in the back by several inches. She turned. Her back was bared almost to the waist, as if the dress had been designed to be seen from the rear.

"It belonged to Lady Diana Woods, when she was Diana Middleton."

Matt stared.

"One of Evelyn Waugh's mistresses," Susan went on. "I bought it from a London dealer."

Matt burst out laughing. "That's the first dress I've seen with a curriculum vitae. I just hope I'm up to it. These briefs," he added, gesturing, "were marked down at Eaton's."

"Then I'm not sure we should have dinner together."

"We'll cope." Matt slid his finger along the material's edge, moving slowly down Susan's back and half touching her skin; she shivered. "I look forward to watching you undress later."

In the dining room they were shown to another window table, as Matt had requested. They were filled with the promise of this lovely wet amorous night. Bowls of late-summer roses, flickering candles, stylish men and women. Matt touched Susan's hand and they resumed staring into each other's eyes. A waiter recommended the chilled vichyssoise, and salmon collops, a speciality. Well-being flickered from table to table, like the candlelight. Cocktails arrived.

A woman's shrill voice pierced the air. "Why did you bring me here?"

Susan and Matt looked toward a table nearby and saw the elegant fiftyish couple from the lounge.

"I couldn't tell you at home. I tried to but I could never . . ."

"And you'd throw away twenty-three years for some poopsie?" she yelled, pushing her chair back from the table. Then she grabbed a wicker basket of rolls and smacked his head with it, rolls flying in all directions. He sat as she hit him again and again. "You bring me . . . up here . . . to say this . . ." Down came the basket. "The dumb ones . . . always . . . fuck best . . ."

The maître d' appeared instantly, followed by a wine steward, as an audible hush fell over the restaurant. Possibly half a dozen couples watched.

"Carl!" the woman shouted, and then fell sobbing against the maître d', who led her away as if returning an overdone filet to the kitchen. Forks and knives went back to work. The husband set his napkin aside, took a deep breath and followed the wine steward.

Matt thought of Ruth, Susan of Seth. Everyone had somebody to recall, and that was that. People selected cheese, lit cigarettes. Matt reached for his martini and sipped. "Mm."

"Well, Matt," Susan said, taking a lighter from her fringed handbag. He reached for a book of matches in the china ashtray, still bothered about his afternoon speech. Maybe I'm not really a moralist, Matt thought. Maybe I'm just tired.

Susan drew his hands toward her as he held out a burning match. "I understand the chef buys most of his vegetables from local farms," Matt explained in his calm professional voice. Susan blew smoke through her nose.

For no clear reason, she felt her eyes start to cloud with tears. "I should change to menthol," Susan said.

Mercifully a waiter came by for their order.

"We had a bad moment there," Matt reflected when they were alone again. "You're very beautiful."

The night and its promise wouldn't fool them for long.

"My father was a Rosicrucian and a theosophist," Susan began. I'm not going to start on this one, she thought, with a rush of panic. "He had a mirror in the attic where he'd do all his reading, or experiments. Whatever they do. His friends would come over—they were all vegetarians, too, and spent hours at the same health-food store, which was pretty weird back then—and they talked forever in that attic. I was being religious then, I was maybe eight or nine, and when my father got cancer I thought he was being laid low for straying from the faith, the way they teach you." Matt listened attentively, perhaps feigning interest, Susan feared, but she continued. "Now that I'm older I'd like to know what the hell was going on in our attic."

"You never asked?"

Susan shook her head. "Once I looked up Rosicrucian in the dictionary." She paused as the waiter brought their salads. Poor Matt took it well, being nailed to the spot with her biography. Whenever she'd told stories to Seth, he'd said, "I don't want to be your therapist." Finally she'd replied, "Some days I forget you for almost an afternoon."

"I'm sorry." Susan hesitated, turning over a spin-

114

ach leaf with her fork. "One of my rules is never to empty out pockets of history like this. I don't know what got into me."

"While you were talking, I saw how I do the same thing."

A truce settled over them, wine, food, flowers, candles coming back to the fore as rain pounded the window. If love couldn't flourish here, their waiter seemed to imply, placing a whole trout before Matt and skilfully deboning it with a quick flip of knife and wrist, then you had only yourself to blame. Susan's salmon required less attention, so her conscience had a rest. A taste of trout? Try the sauce, too. There. But you didn't get any of these little potatoes, you got rice. They felt an odd loss of self.

More wine, brandy at the table, another upstairs in their room, undressing, soft pillows. Matt flipped on the bedside FM to Billie Holiday singing *All of me*. He flipped it off. Atoms, again.

Unable to sleep, each shifted position, rolled over, tossed, bumped into the other, drew close, pulled away.

"It's too hot to sleep with someone," Matt said.

"Don't try so hard."

"It's too hot."

"We could turn up the air-conditioner."

"Maybe I should take a pill," he groaned back.

"Yes. Can I get it?"

"You'd never find them." He paused, moving toward her. "Do you like word games?"

"Not really," Susan answered.

They fell silent for a while.

"I wonder what time it is."

Something fell to the floor.

"Keep your eyes closed and I'll look." Susan turned on the beside lamp: Matt had an arm over his eyes.

"Four-thirty."

"Oh god. Maybe we could phone up all the people we hate in common."

Susan laughed. "They'd think someone died."

"I should take that pill . . ." Six months ago Ruth had grabbed her amber necklace, his present last Christmas, and ripped if from her neck, beads falling over her dress. Matt hadn't been able to move. Then she'd taken a handful of beads and flung them into his face, shouting "Divorce! Divorce!"

Susan leaned over, kissing his chin. "I don't think there's anything I wouldn't let you do to my body."

"There are at least ninety-three things." He laughed.

"Name one."

"We've already tried several."

"Tell me another, then."

"I don't want to shock you."

"Oh yeah?"

Burying his face in Susan's shoulder, he whispered "Hullo there."

"Matt?"

He pulled away. "Let me read to you. I like reading to women." He reached for a book on her bedside table, *Cambodian Torture, an Inquiry by Amnesty International.* Flipping through it, Matt stopped: "Dr. Levenson's examinations showed that fourteen women . . ."

"No!" Susan grabbed the report from him.

"You don't think I have much of a social conscience, right?"

"Let's not . . ."

"Torture's such a nice clean subject—everyone can feel indignant."

"Stop it, Matt."

"You just don't like to admit what's inside people.

If it weren't for torture, I'd have to shut down practice."

"It's made you callous."

Matt grabbed Susan, tickling her back. "Come on, now."

"Men are pigs," she laughed.

He flipped off the lamp and snuggled against her. "Ssh."

Only the restaurant's window tables were set for breakfast.

"We can have a swim." Matt rustled a morning paper taken from the lobby.

Susan looked out at a slope of lawn beyond the garden, then up into a tentative sun. "Yes, we should." The kippers in milk she'd ordered suddenly appeared ominous. Matt had already phoned his answering service, and she wanted to make something right between them.

"Then it's settled." He poured more tea. What made him feel embarrassed? Susan's romanticism—that must be it. "You even wake up beautiful," he added. It wasn't fair to say that, Matt thought.

An hour later they had the pool to themselves. Susan watched Matt dive. She always hated the moment when someone learned that she could only float, and years of exasperation, high-school tears, dates refused, stirred in her as Matt made his graceful way back and forth across the pool. "Come on in," he called.

"Too cold for me."

After several more lengths, Matt pulled himself out of the pool and sat beside Susan, who took up a towel to rub his head.

"Susan," he laughed, clasping her hands, "I'm going back in." He stood up, stretched, took a breath and dove.

The moment held a fraction too long, and then

another moment. Susan screamed. Matt didn't break the water's surface. She kept screaming.

A young man in jogging shorts, one of yesterday's waiters, ran up behind her and instantly jumped in the pool.

After some splashing, the two men emerged.

"That's never happened before." Matt gasped for air as he lay on his back. Susan touched a small red bruise on his forehead.

"You might have a concussion, we'd better . . ."

"No, Susan, I'm fine. I just hit bottom. I just hit bottom."

Several guests wandered toward the pool as the waiter said "I'll call a doctor for you."

Susan felt a cloud move over the sun. "Accidents are . . ."

"There's no such thing as an accident," Matt interrupted.

"Oh, Matt. For god's sake."

"That's the core of my work, my training." He pressed her hand with a kind of useless regret.

Now that the sun was gone, the air felt cold.

They wouldn't see each other again, though neither mentioned it.

Notes on Parking

Night is a shadow. When it falls you could almost think it a miracle, if you believed in miracles any more. City block, church, school, house, become as one. Not one, but as one. And since we're told this is a fallen world, nobody seems to mind very much.

I wait around a lot for things to happen. Waiting like this makes you full, heavy, like a water-logged sponge that's sat too long on the edge of the bathtub. Naturally waiting at night's the worst. No miracle this time, you're sure; not today. The upshot is simple: I've developed an allergy to night. Not as basic as insomnia, nothing in the category of bad dreams, nightmares, upset stomach from overeating. No, it's like this—long about nine o'clock my nose starts to block up, I sniffle, feel a cold coming on. This can be annoying at parties, at dinners with friends—the place doesn't matter. I even block up in movies and concerts where there's no outside darkness to see. This makes me believe the allergy is to night itself, to night and the absence of miracle.

Occasionally I decide to do something about this. Consulting doctors and allergy specialists has cost me weeks of salary to no avail. The problem is in my head.

"Is it a raccoon?"

119

"No. A bird of some sort."
Silence between us.
"Oh."
The noise in the leaves keeps on.
"Just a bird."

We are beyond the old green and white tennis clubhouse, its wire fence, empty parking lot; beyond the park's vast lawn with men sunning and a few women watching children; beyond even the start of the creek, down in the bottom of the ravine, by the rocks where small clumps of wood violets grow. Green and brown everywhere. Dark twigs, leaves half open, small and tender. A yellow forsythia blooms colour by the edge of the creek and here and there on the steep wooded hillsides behind and in front of us.

Silence. We continue to watch the leaves, dried-out ground cover from last fall, where the bird flutters about.

Enough sun comes through the trees to keep us warm. In another few weeks, another month, the leaves will be full and this point in the ravine darker, cooler, misty.

Comments overheard when new people arrive and spread out their towels, or when those already here shift around, turn over, light cigarettes:

"He showed up excessively well dressed."

"Last night I counted and since Christmas I've played cribbage at least five hours a day." (It is now mid-June.)

"What pre-tt-t-y feet I have." (He is perhaps twenty-five.)

"My mother always said the same thing when we were little." Laughter.

After standing beside me for five minutes, during which we stare at each other intermittently, he takes a wad of gum from his mouth and sticks it on a branch of the nearby tree. "Saving it for later," he says with a smile.

If you want a convenient label for me, just say I'm a mind divided against itself, like everyone else.

"You're supposed to wear a whistle if you come at night. Because of teen gangs."

We listen attentively. Sympathetically.

"And use it if there's trouble."

"Sisterhood is power," slurs a lithe twenty-year-old wearing a Mickey Mouse tee-shirt.

This breaks us all up.

A man walks by, opening his shirt, and everyone knows he's had a hair transplant and claims that it cost fourteen thousand dollars. But I know this isn't true because a neighbour in my building goes to the same specialist, and the operations cost only seven thousand. Inflationary rhetoric is common.

The park has several entrances. One past the tennis court, as I said before, and another from the north end of the ravine. You get to this by a small street of old houses, which is directly off the city's largest main drag. On the corner of this street there's a McDonald's. This is worth noting because it explains why, among the ravine's hillsides, and in the waist-high bush, purple wild flowers I can't name and tiny wild roses out of an Elizabethan miniature, you often spot empty containers for Big Macs.

On a hot summer night there may be as many as two

hundred men in the ravine searching for something.

The system of pathways is elaborate and tricky if you aren't familiar with it. Once I saw that someone had come along and tied thin wire ropes from tree to tree, about five inches off the ground. I undid as many as I saw and cut the skin on my hand tearing one of them.

This is my first year as a regular, but I come in the days. The night-time is enough to send me sneezing and snorting so badly that I scare everyone away. But imagine this: a full moon casting pale light as you walk into the darkest blue, the darkest green, so dark they are almost black, but the soft, warm, inviting black of trees, bushes, weeds and thistles and wildflowers as high as your waist, and so dense there are no pathways worn through them this early in the summer.

One friend—well, in fact only an acquaintance— claims to prefer the park at night because darkness turns it into a paradise. If anyone asks his name, he tells them Adam. It's actually Gary, and he teaches high-school English.

Two men in cutoffs walk by my towel and of course I look up at them. Both are shirtless, though one wears an old leather vest. He says, much annoyed, "All the trees blooming, flowers blooming, every fucking thing in the natural world blooming except my life."

Ten minutes later a man looking like Richard Chamberlain as young Dr. Kildare saunters by whistling "Send in the Clowns." This brings an immediate atmosphere of regret, as if the lawn itself were sighing with memories. A few people glance at each other from towel to towel.

Someone laughs. "Nobody goes to that bar unless he's over thirty, I mean, don't you know it's called the Open Grave?"

I turn on my towel, which has begun to smell pleasantly of sweat and Coppertone, and imagine a paragraph in a book written two hundred years from now: "During the middle of the twentieth century it became fashionable to change the colour of one's skin. This was done by the aid of solvents that encouraged the skin to burn when exposed to the sun for prolonged periods of time. Whole industries developed for the manufacture and distribution of these solvents. . . ." There are small, nearly invisible flies in the freshly mown grass. There is also a bee, perhaps the same one that bothered me yesterday.

If someone passes by and you find him appealing, just slip your cutoffs over your swim trunks and follow, pretending to admire the foliage while waiting for an almost imperceptible sign. Do not whistle admiration, and watch for bits of broken glass from beer bottles. You may feel conspicuous the first time you head into the trees, but everyone here understands.

"Lead on," I say to the man who catches my eye by the drinking fountain. I wonder if he'll tell me his name, later. The underbrush scratches our legs.

Overheard on a pathway through elderberry bushes: "Phil says I'm always carrying a wedding veil over my arm."

The man I follow turns, then smiles reassuringly. Neither of us wants to be a bride.

Afterward we talk of this and that. He teaches a course called "Man and Society" in one of the better suburban high schools. "Civics made relevant," he jokes.

The park is full of teachers during the day.

"Can I have your number?" he asks.

"Sure, if you'll give me yours too."

"Well, you see, I live with my lover. We've been together for eight years and there's one rule—we don't give out phone numbers."

"Oh."

Silence. Leaves shadow patterns across his chest and shoulders.

"You understand?"

"Sure." I nod.

"I'd really like to see you again."

"I wouldn't use the number."

He smiles affably. "I don't want to throw away eight years for a phone number."

"I understand. It's just that it never feels reciprocal unless I get a number too."

He shrugs, still affable. "I'm not into reciprocity."

Things to bring to the park:

If you have a burlap shoulder bag (most army surplus stores sell them), pack a towel rolled up, cigarettes and matches, just matches if you don't smoke, suntan lotion or oil, or cocoa butter, which I think people use because it sounds nice, perhaps some fruit, munchies and a book. I've seen guys bring beer and cold cans of pop.

Or, just roll up your towel after placing the lotion and matches on it. People who carry towels seldom bring books.

Though it's not a hard-and-fast rule, transistor radios are generally frowned upon.

While I'm lying here, only a mile away in any direction

immigrant children are being given the means of social mobility, psychiatrists order electro-shock treatments and ministers write their Sunday sermons. The city goes on. I brush some dried grass from my shoulder, then run my hand over the hairs on my chest.

Radiant or tired or bored faces watch the promenade. By now it's July, and confidences get shared from towel to towel; summer bonds have been made. I can't help but notice eyes. Our expressions too careful, guarded, as the cliché would have it. One thing about eyes, they leave you free to imagine: Is he planning a special dinner, weighing the possibilities of chicken Marengo against poached salmon, or rehearsing the argument that will end five monogamous years? Perhaps neither. But surely that one is debating about a new pair of running shoes, or is it which movie he'll see tonight on the second date? It often seems that we are all lonely together.

"You're married?" I ask.
        "No. Why?"
        "The wedding ring."
        Both of us stare down at the plain gold band he's wearing.
        "My grandfather's. I used to have his pocketwatch, too, until some trick stole it."
        A sympathetic sigh from me.
        "So I figure as long as I keep the ring on nobody can get it."

Overheard as I enter the park by log steps set into the hillside: "Then what kind of exercises do you do?"

Farther along I pass two men in the bushes, one on his

knees before the other, and resist the temptation to hum a few bars of "Strangers in Paradise." I believe the man kneeling is a freelance writer who recently finished the text for a coffee-table book about angels. It will have almost two hundred photographs, twenty in full colour.

Even the day's most unimportant moments can be re-called later on as a warning. I continue to make my way through paths along the creek, pushing branches aside when necessary, and finally come to a clearing under the bridge that supports a city street above the ravine. I look up at the mass of stone and concrete, and hear traffic rush by. This is where you can cross the creek most easily because enough large rocks stand out as stepping stones. The bridge overhead keeps this spot especially cool and dank; air seems dirty here. I cross, reach the cement embankment and notice a dead raccoon. Pathways con-tinue to the edge of the woods, where trees meet grass. After surveying the lawn to choose a place for my towel, I realize no one is talking, no one crouches beside a friend, sharing a match. I unroll my towel, spread it out and slip off my jeans. A man on the towel nearest mine appears to be reading a mystery novel called *Danger Waters*, but in fact only stares at the same page, without even bothering to turn it. When I finally lie down, he looks over at me and says, "Two guys were beaten here last night. Possibly one of them's dead."

I promise not to think about it—nothing can be done. Instead, I rub oil on my shoulders, arms, chest, stomach, legs. Wipe my hands so they don't smudge grease stains on the library book I'm going to read. Sun beats down and the oily hairs on my body glisten. Against the deep tan they appear brown, even golden, but along the thin, paler strip of thigh at the edge of my swimtrunks, the hairs are dark, almost black. I roll over on my stomach, trying not to fall asleep and forget about the sun.

Days pass like this. I miss a week in late July when my parents visit. We eat too much and spend time at the zoo. Mother breads chicken for some of my friends while I dream about the park. Is my tan already fading?

Nobody died after all; just one broken nose and some bruises.

Dog days. Cicadas hiss their ugly electric sound. The air-conditioner in my apartment breaks; I can't repair it. Sweat beads everyone's forehead.

Wild asters open down in the ravine, and prickly thistles bulge with lavender heads. Yet the colours seem tired from the heat, and tanned to a deeper gold, a deeper red. The ground is seldom damp, and dry paths clearly marked from footsteps. Most Queen Anne's lace has withered.

On my way to the park I buy an ice-cream bar, fold back the wrapper and bite it. The cold hurts my teeth.

There is a Presbyterian church on the corner opposite McDonald's, and each week its minister selects another inspirational passage to be carefully lettered on a large piece of cardboard that is set into a glass case on the church's lawn. I stop and read:

Summer is over
The harvest is in
And You are not saved

The sentiment seems premature.

One thing I haven't mentioned is the anticipation that grows as you walk toward the ravine. It's a heady emotion, and when you step down the long stairs into the trees, and feel their cool shade, this state of mind is waiting to hold you for several hours.

At about four-thirty this afternoon I feel a sense of dread, but unfocused, troubling. I scratch the mosquito-bite on my wrist and look directly into the sun. The light turns black. I close and open my eyes yet nothing changes. The sky's still a clear blue, cloudless, with no hint of rain. I remember being caught in the ravine during an early summer shower. People stood under the bridge or scurried home while rain pelted and the leaves above us spun dark with water. This is different. I look into the sun again and understand that the days are growing shorter.

For the first time several regulars wear sweatshirts instead of tee-shirts.

Overheard somewhere between the drinking fountain and the tennis court: "The trouble is, you have to stand around buying drinks you don't want. At least here I don't need to spend a cent."

I wake up sniffling. The air in my room is chilly, so I pull on a terrycloth robe and go into the kitchen and make tea. I find peanut butter and spread some on a slice of bread, then take my sandwich into the living room, where I've left my cigarettes. Lighting one, I look out the window at the sky, at trees and buildings black against it. Why do the songwriters say the night was made for love? I smoke one cigarette after another, wondering how many people are in the park now, in the middle of the night. Funny that we don't have a word for it—just middle of the night. There's sunrise, dawn, noon, twilight or dusk, each a precise time, not clock time but still definite. Middle of the night can mean almost anything you want. I wonder if Adam's out in it now, waiting for the miracle.

Hide and Seek

Alex had been with us for nearly two weeks, and I still hadn't satisfied my curiosity about his gloved hand, when Grandpa and Grandma started whispering to my parents. (We had renamed him Alex, for Sandor, just as we changed his brother Laszlo into Leslie.) My grandparents usually spoke Hungarian for secrets—I knew a dozen words, and numbers up to twenty—but with Alex and Les around, they had to use English, and whispering.

"The clowns," Grandpa now called them, when they were out of sight, and even a nine-year-old like me could hear his disappointment. "You have to get jobs," he'd say each night at dinner. "I left Hungary in 1903. I know. That's what you do first."

"I'll wait," Les replied, cutting his meat while my folks stared. "At home there was no such thing as begging for work. At home men would see me and take their hats off and say 'Good afternoon, *tanitó-úr*.'" (Later Grandma said it meant "sir teacher"—two more words.) "If you're a teacher, all you do is walk into the movie-house, they know who the teachers are, they never charge you."

Les had taught Latin in Gyor, outside Budapest, where his father owned a restaurant in which Alex, a year younger, had worked. Both were in their mid-twenties, Les tall and fair, with Grandpa's sharp blue eyes and

131

beaky nose, and Alex—the one I liked best—shorter, stockier, with dark brown hair, fine features and an artificial right hand covered by a black leather glove. Though it was summer when he came to us, Alex always wore long-sleeved shirts. The hand kept perfectly still, except for a movable thumb that Mother said helped him hold onto things. I never saw him use it, though. Whenever I got a chance at dinner, I'd pass him bread, or butter, always toward his right, but the hand stayed in his lap, or on the edge of the table.

"You think somebody's going to appear at the house, knock on the door, and say 'Come on, work'?" Grandpa asked. "Well maybe in Europe. Over here, you want to eat, you got to work. You want to work, you got to find a job."

Les and Alex would look at each other, then down at their plates. Sometimes I caught a twitch in Alex's lips, as if he was trying not to smile.

Russian tanks had rolled into Hungary on my last birthday, and since then I'd imagined Les and Alex as freedom fighters. I'd even bragged at school that one of my Budapest cousins was shot in the arm. But around Christmas Grandpa's brother wrote saying that his sons, quiet, sensible boys, hoped to find their fortunes in the new country. With this letter came a recent family snapshot. Someone had drawn a thin red line at Alex's wrist, by the glove's edge.

"Did the Russians do that?" I asked, thinking about air-raid drills at school when we walked single file to the basement, bent down on one knee, covered our heads and tried not to giggle.

"No," Mother explained. "When he was a boy, he found a grenade left over from the war. He didn't know what it was, so he picked it up and it exploded and blew off his hand."

"That's all?" I blurted out.

"Oh, it's worse to be crippled as a child because of some grown-ups' war."

"They're good boys," added Grandpa.

"Will they really come here?" My family often talked about refugees, but the snapshot helped me to picture them. Their clothes seemed either too big or too long, and on one of the children I spotted an old sweater of mine. Twice a year Grandpa sent care packages filled with clothes bought on sale and our little-worn discards.

"Don't talk about them to your friends," Grandpa warned.

On the day school let out for summer vacation, Les and Alex arrived.

"Why do I have to leave them alone?"

Mother set a glass of orange juice in front of me. "Just in the morning, Bob."

"But why?"

Though we shared a double house with Mother's parents, who lived upstairs, the family really split between Grandma and Mother on one side and Grandpa and Father, sort of, on the other. The woman side always answered questions.

"Grandpa wants to help them find jobs," she went on.

"Couldn't Les teach at my school?" Trying to imagine this, I saw it wouldn't work. He knew nothing American. The other night he'd asked about a book I was reading, *The Clue of the Hissing Serpent*, and had never even heard of the Hardy boys.

"There are a lot of refugees now," Mother continued, buttering toast, "so it's hard to find work." She explained how Grandpa had tried to get them in as orderlies at the local hospital, as waiters at restaurants he liked or into jobs in the company where he'd worked before retiring. "And they don't speak much English." She shook her head.

"That's why I'm teaching Les." He'd read several pages of the Hardy boys aloud while I corrected his pronunciation. I'd rather have helped Alex, but he didn't seem to like books. I never saw him with one. Les, who was starting night-school English classes, read all the time.

"Just don't bother them during the day."

"But they don't like going out with Grandpa."

"Who told you that?"

"I just know." I tapped a jar of Grandma's home-made jam with my spoon.

"Don't worry so much about them. What are you doing today?"

"Do you really think Les climbed over a barbed-wire fence into Austria?" Lean and athletic, Les would come into the backyard, pull off his shirt and do handstands, showing me how. I could imagine him escaping in the night.

Mother sipped coffee without answering.

"And once he got into Austria he was okay."

"They've had a bad time, we should let them forget it."

"But Alex, how did he get over the fence? With that hand."

"If you've finished breakfast, why don't you go out and play."

I lay low for a while and then sneaked upstairs, hoping to catch sight of my cousins. Maybe Grandpa would give them a day off. Instead I found Grandma alone in the living room, making up the sofa and cot where Les and Alex slept. Her eyes were bright with anger.

"Everyone's out already, Grandma?"

She nodded and went on folding blankets.

Grandma and Grandpa didn't like each other. They had separate bedrooms and wouldn't even eat breakfast at the same table.

"What's the matter, Gram?"

"Oh, him," she mumbled, then came over and put her arms around me.

"I forgot to give you this," Mother said, handing Les a thin blue aerogram as Grandma cleared dinner plates. Father, impatient to wash his car, glared at the letter. Grandpa seemed glum, maybe expecting bad news. Before dinner he'd whispered something to Mother about "walking their legs off."

Les took out a photograph of a young girl in evening dress and long white gloves, holding a spray of roses. She seemed foreign, with sad eyes and her hair in a funny knob on the top of her head, which she held very straight, as if the knob might fall off. On the back of the picture, a few handwritten words. "Look at that," Les said, passing the picture to his brother. "What a thing to write to me."

Alex took the picture and read aloud something I didn't understand. Both Mother and Grandma stopped scraping dishes and peered over his shoulder at the photograph.

"What does it mean?" I asked.

"Nothing," Grandpa answered.

"Then tell me."

"I can translate," Alex said, examining the picture. "Les had a girlfriend, and this is her . . . how do you call it . . ."

"Graduation," Mother answered.

"Graduation," he repeated. "From college. She writes, 'Dear Laci, please come home, let us grow old together. With all my love, Katya.'"

"What a thing to write to a man," Les exclaimed.

"I think it's the most beautiful thing I ever heard," said Mother.

"It is very bad," Alex agreed with his brother.

Mother shook her head slowly. "How her heart must ache, knowing she'll never see you again."

Les started to laugh and my father pushed back his chair. "Come on," he said in my direction. "You can polish the bumpers."

I spent a long time polishing and gradually dusk fell. A warm breeze smelled of roses. Almost hidden by tall stalks of larkspur, Grandma weeded her flower garden, while Grandpa and Mother staked tomatoes beside the garage. Shirtless as usual, Les stood in the middle of the lawn, bouncing a soccer ball off his head and then catching it. Every few minutes Grandpa glanced toward the kitchen windows.

"See how high it goes," Les said, and the ball went up at least fifteen feet.

Grandma burst out laughing. "Oh you make my head hurt."

"Uncle, remember you sent us a camera and that football? We didn't know what to do with it. We played soccer."

It was funny to hear Grandpa called Uncle. He didn't answer.

"Do you like football?" Les asked, turning to me.

He now rolled the ball over his left shoulder, across the neck, onto the right shoulder and down his arm. I wondered what Alex was doing. He spent a lot of time upstairs by himself.

"Hey," I cried. A firefly, then two, three, a dozen, began flashing.

"Tüzbogár," said Les.

"Lightning bug," I said. "Or firefly."

He grinned. *"Szentjánosbogár*—St. John's bug. At home we put them in jars, and made holes in the lids, so they could breathe. Want to catch them?"

Mother came over and said, "Not tonight. It's getting late."

Without arguing I went off to my room to finish *The Flickering Torch Mystery.* Soon I heard voices on the front porch. Like a good detective, I stole into the living room and hid by an open window. Alex had joined them and everyone sat talking softly in the dark. They switched back and forth from Hungarian to English, laughing easily—even Grandpa. I knew the men were drinking beer. "Oh, no, that's terrible," Mother said as Les's voice rose a bit over the others. "You learn to love with old ladies, not young ones," he continued. "Just like if you ride a bicycle, you don't get a new one and ride it, you get an old one first." "Sssh," Grandma said, and Grandpa mumbled something in Hungarian. My father breathed disapproval. "That's terrible," repeated Mother, yet she was laughing.

Over the weekend Grandpa's whispering stopped. "They bum all day or sleep all day," he complained. Watching Mother peel potatoes for supper, he didn't seem to mind that I sat at the kitchen table with a new Archie comic. "He came here thinking he'd have everyone bowing down to him. *Tanitó-úr.*" Grandpa nearly spat the words.

"They're trying," Mother said, something sad in her voice. "And what can Alex do, with that hand?"

This was the first time she'd mentioned it.

"I'm buying all the food, they don't have a nickel. But they go out and drink with their friends."

"It's nice they've made friends," she interrupted.

Two guys in their twenties had come to the door for Les a couple of times. They spoke Hungarian and slapped him on the shoulder. Les never introduced us, but he and Alex disappeared for the evening in their battered Chevy.

"Nice? What's nice about it? I tell them, jobs first."

"Maybe they don't like us any more," I suggested.

"Go, read your book on the porch." He didn't sound angry, just impatient.

"Take a cookie," said Mother, "and then practise your scales."

Closing the screen door, I heard Grandpa ask, "What else can I do?"

We planned a real Fourth of July for Les and Alex, with hamburgers barbecued outside and corn on the cob. I told Alex as we sat on the front porch before supper, and he described the wood stove his mother used. "At home, no electricity, no gas." It sounded like a history book. When I explained what hamburgers were, he looked disappointed. Corn on the cob, he said, they fed to the pigs.

"Don't you like it here?" I asked, looking right at him as we swung back and forth on the glider.

"Yes." He seemed to think for a minute. "Yes."

"Do you know any good secrets?"

"Secrets aren't good," he answered slowly. The

way he said it made me feel grown-up.

We kept on swinging. "I could teach you to play Parcheesi," I offered. "But tonight there's fireworks."

As we talked, the old Chevy pulled into our yard. Alex stood up and in a second Les appeared. "We'll be back," he called, settling into the car. Alex waved with his good hand.

Father had promised to take us to see fireworks, but with no sign of Alex or Les, supper was late. "Let's wait," I said, "they'll be here in time." Grandpa muttered something and told my father to start the fire. "I don't want to go without them," I grumbled. We ate quickly and went off to the park, leaving Grandpa behind.

Explosions of red, white, yellow and blue swooped through the sky—without my cousins. Maybe I'd spoiled everything by telling Alex.

"Get away from there," Mother said, her face red. "Right now."

"But Ma . . ." I stood near our hall door, listening. The fireworks upstairs were almost as good as the ones last night.

"You don't care about anything," shouted Grandpa.

"Shut that door," Mother said, though I knew she wanted to listen too.

"I promised my brother I'd look after you . . ."

We'd just started breakfast when I heard Grandpa again. Les and Alex had come in around three in the morning, and he'd waited up for them on the dark porch.

". . . but you're just a couple of clowns."

Someone ran across the kitchen above us. A door slammed.

For a moment there was no sound, then the hall door opened again.

139

"Come back till I'm finished!"

Footsteps pounding down the hall stairs. I pulled back just as another door slammed.

Mother and I got to a window in time to see the guys stomp out of the yard.

After breakfast I biked up East Boulevard looking for Alex and Les. No sign of them anywhere. Discouraged, I stopped by the high school to watch a baseball game. How lucky—to be grown up, in high school. But then I got bored and rode around again, dropping into the library for another Hardy boys. I looked at all the titles—*The Witchmaster's Key*, *Footprints under the Window*—and thought maybe I could write one. *The Mystery of the Gloved Hand*. Only there wasn't much mystery in it. By now it was lunchtime. I didn't know where else to look.

Getting off my bike by the back porch, I saw two people behind the low fence between Grandma's flowers and the vegetable garden. The tops of two heads, two heads of fair curls through the larkspur that covered the fence. Mother and Les kneeling in the garden. "Hey," I called.

Les stood first and brushed dirt from his pants. Then he bent to Mother, put his hands out and helped her up, like one of those paper flowers that rise from a shell when you drop them in water. He held onto her hands for a minute.

I ran into the kitchen, where Grandma was rolling out a pie crust. "I told them you'd be home for lunch," she said.

Mother followed me in, carrying a colander full of strawberries. Without asking where I'd been, she went to the sink and began examining them, as if she expected to find a pearl or something. "Les has a job," she announced.

"At a chemical company. He'll clean out paint vats . . ."

"That's terrible," Grandma sighed.

Mother started washing berries.

"I was so lonely when I came here." It never took much to get Grandma going on the old country. "They must miss their parents. I remember . . ."

"And he's found a roominghouse for them."

"They're good boys."

Mother finally turned off the faucet. "Do you know where your wedding pictures are? It struck me that Les's the spitting image of Pa when you got married."

"What are you talking about?" Grandma asked, frowning at her pie crust. "I'm not married."

We knew to ignore this.

"Maybe they're up in the attic. It would be fun to show them tonight."

"Alex should see the pictures too," Grandpa suggested. On the front porch warm evening air made all of us lazy, and the photograph album sat unopened in Mother's lap. The women and I drank iced tea, the men, beer. Occasionally Grandpa let me sip from his glass, so I knew there'd been a truce. Now he only had to worry about finding a job for Alex.

"He should see them," Mother agreed.

Les and Alex were moving out on the weekend, in four days. "I'll get him," I offered, still curious about the time he spent alone, without books or anyone to talk to. I wondered what would happen to Alex at the roominghouse.

Careful not to make a sound, I went up the hall stairs. No light had been turned on and shadows filled the house. It seemed darker here than out on the porch, and felt sort of creepy. Tiptoeing into the dining room, I could make out an open suitcase, with clothes folded in it, and others draped over a chair. Alex sat on the cot beside the sofa, his back to me, his head hanging forward. He'd taken off his shirt and his skin looked olive-coloured, like mine, not fair, like Les's. About a foot away from him on the cot lay the black-gloved hand, as if it didn't belong to anyone. Hard to make out in the poor light, it had some leather straps hooked onto it.

"Alex," I whispered.

He didn't move. I heard him moan, or clear his throat, and wanted to run.

"Alex?"

He made another choking sound and then began to pull himself up. I took a few steps toward him and saw the bad arm hanging there, ending in a stump.

"We thought . . ."

His shoulders fell again.

"Alex."

And when he turned, I saw he'd been crying.

"I'm sorry." I pulled back. "I didn't mean . . ." and I kept backing away as he looked into my eyes. Another step, another, and I bumped against the dining-room table. I couldn't look away. Another step, one more, and I was in the kitchen. I could still see him staring over his shoulder, hardly breathing.

Covered with goose bumps, I hurried downstairs and kept on going, to the basement, easing the door shut behind me. I went into the fruit cellar where Grandma stored pickles and jam, and sat on an old orange crate. I'd never seen a man cry, and now I was glad Les and Alex were leaving us. The weekend seemed too far away.

I sat there for a while. One of the window panes had been painted over, but the other let in just enough light for me to see my hands.

Then, a voice—Les's. I heard my name and

142

another word I didn't catch. He repeated it. "The fire-flies . . . fireflies."

I tried not to listen.

"I punched holes in a jar, like at home."

I pretended not to hear.

"Where are you? Come on out."

Did he think this a dumb kid's game, hide and seek?

More footsteps past the window. But I couldn't go up. Not till I was ready.

Aunt Helen's Will

"And you know she left the farm to you."

So, I'd reached the age of inheritance. That time of life when people suddenly buy Corvettes or visit Tahiti. For me, a drafty brick farmhouse ten miles outside Chagrin Falls, Ohio. Built in 1850, it had been a slave stop on the underground railroad, a county landmark of sorts. Aunt Helen used to say, "I must've painted every damn tree in these woods." But she loved nothing more than that farm, not even her paintings.

Ma was reminiscing. Both the Kissel girls had been beauties, popular Catholic brunettes. After high school, Ma worked as a secretary for a building contractor, my father-to-be; on weekends they danced to touring big bands. A year younger, Aunt Helen started art school but dropped out to marry. Not long after, World War II made her a widow and she found a job at American Greeting painting birthday-card flowers. On weekends she painted for herself. I thought she was Rembrandt.

She taught me how to drive a stick shift, gave me my first martini, my first recording of Beethoven's ninth. Earlier, though, she showed me how to render: eyes focused on an object, you drew its outline, never looking to see the progress of your sketch, the pencil moving slowly, steadily, hand and eyes one.

The old man starts on the "proper books for a teenager" just as we sit down to the Sunday roast. This morning, after mass, he raided my paperbacks. *Peyton Place, The Catcher in the Rye, A Rage to Live.*

"Irene." A pause to let us know this is serious business. "I don't understand why you let him read such trash."

Before Ma answers—you can never really answer him—I come out with "Yassuh," in a slow drawl, like one of Scarlett O'Hara's darkies.

"Trying to be smart?"

"I don't have to try."

"Want to know what my hand feels like? You aren't too big . . ."

Aunt Helen breaks in. "How about if Tom comes to me for the summer vacation?" Just like that, in front of me. Fifteen is rotten.

"To help in the studio—instead of wasting the summer."

Of course there'll be fresh air, fresh eggs, fresh vegetables. We'll probably sit around eating bowls of good fresh country dirt. Then she winks at me.

Summer finally comes. My parents leave me at the farm with looks of relief and regret. But I'm not sorry when Aunt Helen shows me my room, the big one my folks use when we all come for the weekend. It has a worn Turkish carpet and the wicker chairs I helped her paint green.

"That's yours." She points to a wooden box at the foot of the bed. Puzzled, I open it. A palette, brushes, tubes of paint, oil, turpentine.

Helping in the studio actually means cleaning a few brushes. The garden takes more time, especially where vegetables grow in a large plot bordered by raspberry bushes. Every night we eat berries, in pie, on ice cream or just by the handful. Then we play croquet until Aunt Helen has to turn on a yard light. "Got you!" she cries, as her ball cracks against mine, knocking it across the dark lawn. "Letting me win again?"

When I get bored I make like Van Gogh, lugging paints out to the field. It's sunny, hot, the kind of weather people think a big deal. I try everything Aunt Helen suggests but my canvases never look the way I want them to. My arms get streaked with turpentine, and all the birds and nature stuff makes me feel like an idiot. Soon I give up painting and hitch rides into town. There's not much there but the falls, some antique shops, a drugstore. I buy a Coke and hang around until suppertime, thinking mostly about hitching a ride to some place like Santa Fe. I like the sound of Santa Fe. Sometimes I walk down the old wooden steps by the falls—right to the rocks, where you can sit and look into the spray—and if no one's around, smoke a few cigarettes snitched from my aunt. I want summer to be over and I want it never to end.

As executor Ma knew all about the will, planned from the day Aunt Helen phoned to say in a bourbon-soaked voice, "I've got the goddamn big C." Surgery, chemotherapy, morphine followed in grim sequence—grim for my parents, who insisted Aunt Helen move in with them, and for the dying body my aunt became. Whenever I went home to see her we'd talk about it, slugging back Wild Turkey together. She never mentioned the will to me.

One fall afternoon, when smoky October light had subdued the bright leaves, she asked me to drive her to the farm. By the time we got there Aunt Helen was too tired to leave the car. We sat in it, talking—mostly about my classes at the university and my latest book on modern painting. As usual, we didn't talk about that summer twenty-five years before.

"Well, aren't these better than a book?" Aunt Helen asks as we cross the gallery of Renaissance paintings—one holy family after another.

"They ought to be on religious calendars." I'd found a copy of *Lust for Life* in her attic and would have preferred to stay behind when she went into town.

"Just look at this," she says, stopping in front of a murky canvas. The plaque on the frame reads "Adoration of the Magi" and, below, "Titian. Ca 1560. Italian, Venice."

"You really like that?"

"Use your eyes, Tom. If I could have one thing in the museum, just one, this would be it."

"Not me."

"What would you pick?"

"I'll let you know when I find something."

By the end of the afternoon she's won me over.

The following Wednesday, when Aunt Helen goes in to American Greeting, she drops me at the art museum. I keep busy until we meet for lunch, which is really a quiz about my morning with medieval tapestries. Over the cafeteria table I ask, "Wouldn't you like to see one of your paintings hanging here in the gallery?"

She keeps her eyes on her cigarette lighter until it catches. "I'm going to be forty next month." She drags on her cigarette. "By now I know what I can do."

"You're as good as most of those guys."

"I've wasted my talent, honey."

"At least you make money from your painting. Not like Van Gogh."

"Get-well cards." She tosses her head back, blowing

smoke.

I came home with a tie sombre enough for a pallbearer, but Ma greeted me with one of those "nothing's-so-bad-it-can't-get-worse" looks. My aunt had left a letter saying she wanted to be cremated. The ashes were to be buried in the plot she'd bought for her young soldier-husband. A funeral service was forbidden. No prayers, no priests. If we altered her plans, she'd vowed to come back to haunt us.

"She didn't say anything about flowers," Ma said tentatively. "Do you think I could at least leave some flowers?"

We carried out her instructions and were met at the cemetery gatehouse by a small fiftyish man in black topcoat. "I'm Joseph Haas, from Davis Funeral Home." He extended a hand.

"She didn't even hold on till Christmas," Ma whispered, shaking her head as we followed Mr. Haas. It was a rainy December morning, flu weather. Red berries gleamed on the holly bushes that banked the drive winding toward Section M. I remembered coming here after Sunday dinners as a boy. Aunt Helen would bring flowers to her husband's grave and then we'd walk through the old cemetery and its gilded-age obelisks.

As we approached a bend in the road, two men stood with shovels near a familiar gravestone. No one spoke until we reached them. Ma shivered. A burlap bag lay on the ground near a newly dug hole, about two feet deep and eight inches square. Haas bent down, opened the bag and removed a brass urn with Aunt Helen's name engraved across it.

"You're putting it in the ground just like that?" Ma asked. "Not even in a box?"

"It's specially treated metal," he replied. "You can dig it up a hundred years from now and it will still look the same."

"You really want the Pope running the White House?" a fat man asks. But everyone in my aunt's living room ignores him. She's invited a dozen people over to watch the Democratic convention on her new TV—a civics class with potato chips. Kennedy's victory excites everyone but me.

Aunt Helen leans over the back of my chair and whispers, "You don't have to stay up." Her eyes are bright, her face flushed. She's living for the Democratic party tonight. In her black cotton dress and silver Indian jewellery, she's the best-looking woman in the room.

"I'm okay." I slump over my Coke.

Just then the local news comes on. "This afternoon a valuable sixteenth-century print by Albrecht Dürer was stolen from the Cleveland Museum of Art, while visitors walked in and out of the art-filled rooms."

"We were there today!" cries Aunt Helen. "At lunchtime, for god's sake."

A close-up of an empty frame. "Guards found this broken frame in the print room on the ground floor."

I glance up at my aunt. She's staring at the TV.

"At present the police have no leads . . ."

A shot of some blank-faced policemen in the museum's corridors.

Someone switches channels. Noisemakers, balloons, a grinning candidate. I gulp the rest of my Coke. With everyone talking about Kennedy it seems like a good time to leave.

After locking my bedroom door I turn on a lamp, roll back the Turkish carpet and pick up the etching. All through dinner and the party I imagined it there, almost sure I'd made the whole thing up.

I sit on the edge of my bed and stare at the picture. A knight in armour rides along past an old bearded guy with snakes for hair. He must be Death because he's carrying an hourglass and the etching's called, *The Knight, Death and the Devil.* There's a dog running beside the horse, sniffing around, and in the distance, a castle, but far off. The knight's just at the foot of the hill. The Devil looks silly, not frightening. A cross between a donkey and an alligator, with marbles for eyes and a fancy seashell horn. After the knight, the best thing is the dog, though he's got a sort of dumb, rabbity face. On one corner there's a date, 1513, but you don't need that to tell the thing is old.

After the funeral Ma went to bed with some whisky-laced tea, while my dad and I packed Aunt Helen's things in the guestroom.

"Do you want me to call Goodwill?" I asked.

"Destroying the evidence," he said.

Aunt Helen is sitting by an open window, cleaning brushes, when I come into the studio. She looks up and smiles. It strikes me that her features are like Ma's, only somehow put together in a bolder way.

"If you don't have anything to do this afternoon, maybe you'll help me stretch some canvases."

I cross the studio and set the etching on her workbench.

She puts down a brush. "Where'd you get this?" she says, reaching for it. The studio smells of oil and turpentine, heated up by the humid weather. My stomach flips.

"Tom, where'd you get this?"

I keep my eyes on the etching.

"Are you crazy?"

"It was easy. No one's ever around the print room. No guards, nobody. I just took it off the wall, loosened the top of the frame with a quarter and pulled out the print. I used some Kleenex to hold the frame so there wouldn't be any fingerprints."

"How could you do this to me?" Her voice is soft.

I feel her eyes on me and avoid them.

"It rained that day and I had on my windbreaker, so I rolled it up and stuck it in the sleeve."

"But why?"

"They ought to guard things better."

"That's not the point, Tom. You could have been caught . . ."

"I picked a corner of the room where I could see if someone was coming. I'd have heard them anyway."

She puts the etching down, careful to keep it away from her messy brushes.

"At first I had it under the rug in my room, and sometimes I'd take it out, mostly to be sure it was still there. Then I started to hate having it around. If it's so valuable, we could mail it back."

"Why haven't you already done that?" She picks up the print again.

"I thought of going out in the field to burn it . . ."

"Why tell me?"

"I suppose you're going to call my folks."

"First I'll get it back to the museum. You can't drop something like this in the mail."

"They'll crucify me."

"Maybe we won't have to tell them."

"You mean it?"

The countryside looked ready to pose for one of Aunt

Helen's hokier watercolours—snowy roads and farm-houses sporting red-ribboned pine wreaths. In the last decade Chagrin Falls had attracted money and everything was spruced up, full of its own charm. A good place to inherit property.

Driving through the greeting-card scene I began to see the green of the day I'd left her, because she'd been invited to visit friends at Cape Cod.

"I'm sorry, Tom, but we're only cutting your stay short by two weeks."

I shrugged and looked out over the garden. "Sure."

"You don't really mind, do you?"

"I guess you're going because of the print?"

"You know I've taken care of all that." She sounded impatient, but maybe she was just anxious to have her holiday.

"Are you sure you're not going to tell my parents?"

"Tom, I've already told you a dozen times. We don't have to bother them." She picked up a basket of tomatoes and headed for the house.

There'd been no more trips to the museum, and nothing about the Dürer in the papers, only an article on art stolen from museums, giving names and dates back to 1900. I'd expected a fuss when my aunt returned the print, but it wasn't even mentioned. She thought that had something to do with the insurance.

The edge of town, with its ring of fir trees and oaks, gave way to snow-covered fields, and the landscape momentarily changed to a day thirty years earlier, when we'd driven along watching for the painted signs that appeared every hundred feet or so. IF YOU WANT . . . fields of corn . . . A PERFECT SHAVE . . . more corn, pumpkins . . . THEN TRY . . . but no conclusion to the rhyme.

Turning into Aunt Helen's dirt driveway, which became gravel halfway to the house, I thought the farm seemed sad, uninviting. It lacked more than a Christmas wreath. My key stuck in the lock, and I struggled to twist it free before I stepped inside.

The house was bitterly cold. I went into the living room, opened the flue and put on one of the artificial logs she'd begun to use. Its chemical flame burned a lurid turquoise and yellow. Keeping my coat on, I sat at her roll-top desk and looked through the drawers. Monogrammed stationery, a tin box of stamps, a bottle of ink, some bills stamped "Paid."

The old cranberry glass in the dining room was dusty. The buffet drawers held nothing but linens. Upstairs, the guestroom looked as it always had, except the wicker chairs had been painted white. I opened the shutters and saw snow falling on the fields.

In my aunt's bedroom I found the monogrammed envelope in the drawer on her night table. I'd felt sure there'd be a letter and almost guessed its contents. The hand was shaky. "Dear Tom. The farm is yours now. I've been happy here, no matter what anyone thinks. I've had some good times." A new paragraph. "If you don't want my paintings, and your mom and dad haven't room for any more, don't give them away—burn them. Whatever you do, first take them out of their frames. Love, Helen."

Dozens of paintings hung in the house—oils, watercolours, ink drawings. For a start I ruled out anything she hadn't painted, at least half of them, and all the large oils, which were open at the back. Aunt Helen had done most of her own framing, in a pretty makeshift way, so I recognized her work at once.

I pried the cardboard backs loose from two autumn landscapes in the hallway. Nothing under the first, but a watercolour of a bird, almost oriental in its delicacy, under the second. Signed with the familiar HKH. Under an ordinary still-life in one corner of the living room, another watercolour. A single peony, close up, as if she'd been looking at too many Georgia O'Keeffes. HKH again, and 1941.

A half-hour later I'd taken apart most of the paintings on the first floor. The artificial log hadn't done its job, so I went in search of a drink. In the pantry, mouse droppings and a half-bottle of Cointreau. Hardly what I wanted, but I poured a glassful and went upstairs.

I started in Aunt Helen's bedroom with a water-colour of some impressionist garden. The cardboard backing had been taped to the frame, but the tape peeled off in a single dry strip. When the cardboard came loose, a piece of heavy old paper could be seen underneath. I carefully slipped it out and turned over one of the masterpieces of European art.

Even in the dim light it radiated a powerful melancholy. A knight returns from the wars, having seen so much of death that the horrible creature beside him holds no surprise, no terror, just as there will be no comfort for him in the castle. Etched in sure, vigorous lines, he is one of the first absurdists. He rides erect, ignoring the Devil's idiot gaze and the familiar, longed-for road home.

Dusk had fallen and I stood near the window imagining the late quiet nights when she must have taken the etching from its frame, leaned it against her bedside lamp, and sat there, staring.

Throughout the holiday traditions and tensions I tried to be cheerful—the tender sad cheer shared with ageing parents. I had only a few days to solve my Dürer problem before it was time to leave. I pictured the fire, the flood that might destroy it, hanging in the farmhouse as it had for twenty-five years. And should I sell my aunt's farm? Could it become a retreat for me, as it had for her? When Ma asked, I spoke abruptly without meaning to. "I don't have to decide right away, do I?"

Later that day she asked me to go to the cemetery with her. "I'm taking flowers to Helen," she said.

Outside the museum I sat in my car and studied Rodin's *Thinker*. It stood on a block of marble directly in front of the neo-classical entrance. The lower part of the bronze figure had been blown away by a bomb. Student radicals. The poor maimed man seemed to be sitting uncomfortably in mid-air. I sympathized with him.

The Dürer had been rolled into a tube and held in place with a loose rubber band. It fit unnoticeably into the inside pocket of my overcoat, along with a folded manila envelope. After I casually made my way to the director's office, it would be easy to unroll the etching, slip it into the envelope and push it under the door.

As I stepped out of the car, I wondered if she'd expected me to return the etching some day. All those years when I'd asked myself where it was, and never a single word spoken. "Got you," I could hear her saying with a hand of rummy, over the chessboard, as we played croquet.

I took the steps two at a time. The first guard, a middle-aged black man, nodded. When I passed the coat-check I began to relax. Most people were carrying their coats so I took mine off too. The gloves now became a problem—I didn't want to touch the Dürer without them. I took them off.

Had my aunt come to love the Dürer? The small

gallery of Byzantine art was a dead-end. Back to the armour court, with its famous Velasquez. My coat, draped over my arm, felt heavy. I stopped in front of a Rubens, all fat pink valour, and tried to remember the way. Left through the Dutch masters. I hoped she'd loved the etching. Still, I wished she had told me. Concealing it somehow cancelled my act. That one crazy act. Fifteen is rotten.

DIRECTOR, stencilled on the door. I pulled on a glove and felt under the coat. No one in the corridor. Sounds of a typewriter inside the office. My hand began inching the Dürer out of the pocket.

Twenty-five years. So many words spoken, written, read, believed. And now I'd returned to a moment I wanted only to forget.

I pass the Rubens, the Velasquez, the icons and gold reliquaries, and the museum suddenly fills with guards—male, female, old, young. Should I nod to them all? I'm through the lobby, out the door and down the steps, in what seems like a second.

Did my heart pounded like this at fifteen? I can't remember.

In the car I turn on the ignition and take a deep breath as the windshield begins to defrost. I sit back, loosening my coat. I finger Aunt Helen's bequest, still safely rolled up in my pocket. Rodin sits glumly staring at the place where his feet used to be.